BEAUTIFUL NIGHTMARE

A PARANORMAL THRILLER

KINSLEY KINCAID

ISBN eBook: 978-1-998646-12-8

ISBN Paperback: 978-1-998646-11-1

Editing: Rumi Khan

Proofreading: Daisie Mae - Editing & Proofreading

Cover Design: Occult Goddess

Where Darkness Hides.

NOTE FROM THE AUTHOR

Please be aware this book contains many dark themes and subjects that may be uncomfortable/unsuitable for some readers. This book contains **heavy themes** throughout. Please keep this in mind when entering *Beautiful Nightmare*. Content warnings are listed on authors' social pages & website.

This book and its contents are entirely a work of fiction. Any resemblance or similarities to names, characters, organizations, places, events, incidents, or real people are entirely coincidental or used fictitiously.

If you find any genuine errors, please reach out to the author directly to correct it. Thank you.

This book is intended for 18+ only.

PLAYLIST

Numb - Tommee Profitt, Skylar Grey
Clean - Taylor Swift
Is It Really You - Sleep Token, Loathe
Nightmare - Halsey
Dangerous - Sleep Token
vampire diaries - mgk
Famous Last Words - MCR
No Going Home - Heidi Montag
Euclid - Sleep Token
Labyrinth - Taylor Swift

SPOTIFY PLAYLIST

BLURB

It's too deranged to be a dream
But to one, it is beautiful.
Creating fear and possessing souls.
None of this is a figment of imagination.
Everyone involved is very awake, even if they wish they
weren't.
With beating hearts and trembling lips, tranquility no
longer exists.
Because tonight, nightmares become real.
Welcome to Agatha Manor, in Hollows Grove.

1

PRINCE

NEW ORLEANS IN THE 80S - AGE SEVEN

D *ing-dong, can you hear me?*
Can you feel me?
You're going to die. Now, Mommy, die.
Ding-dong, can you see me?
Can you dance off the ledge?
JUMP!

STANDING on top of the roof of our two-story family home, my eyes watch in delight as a cream sleep dress ripples in the air. The bright moon shines down upon us as long black hair billows around her expressionless face and her arms are lifted, not fighting, just falling. The New Orleans night is warm and humid, while the fresh air enters my nose and feeds my lungs.

GOODBYE, *Mommy.*

AND AT THAT EXACT MOMENT, her free fall ends, her body meets the earth, and Mommy's head finds one of the many large decorative stones in our backyard. A single crack echoes as red crimson trickles out of her nose, eyes still wide open. I watch her chest, not blinking once to make sure it is no longer rising with each breath. Smirking once satisfied, my gaze casually moves back to her head, and the same crimson begins to decorate the stone.

Thick gardens surround her, and tall hedges keep the area private; therefore, this is where Mommy will stay to rot.

ROT!

HER EYES BECOME HOLLOW, the whites falling into her sockets and leaving only a black cast. Her skin thins, becoming translucent, while her face caves in and her body deflates. Hundreds of tiny cream maggots crawl out of her orifices. Her eyes become filled with them, while others begin to crawl out of her nose. Long worms hang out of her ears, when I notice Mommy's mouth drop open. You can't see them at first; their long antennas are thin and impossible to identify at night, even with small garden lights illuminating her. But as their wings open, intricate dark gray and black designs mixed with white captivate my vision; beautiful moths begin to surround her. I could get distracted by the vision alone for hours.

Peering past them, I notice the once fresh, glistening blood on the stone is now dark and dried. Mommy's thick raven hair is nothing more than thin strings, and the cream nightgown is tarnished as moths eat away at the silk.

Vines from the garden have laced themselves around her legs, taking her into the fold.

Good riddance to you, Mommy.

I hope you find no peace in death.

As you can no longer give me the shots that suppressed my thoughts, I am finally free.

Your endless need to control only ignited my hatred for you more. Instead of trying to understand the unknown, you suppressed your fear. Me.

An owl hoots; it vibrates through my body. I can feel everything so much more clearly now.

The moths follow, rising with flapping their wings, gathered into a ball of fury above Mommy.

ENOUGH!

THE MOTHS FLOCK TOWARD ME. Their wings tickle my skin as they rush past me in droves. I lift my arms as they pass. A part of me wishes they could take me with them, lift me high above the ground, and float away. But my work here is still not complete.

The cooling breeze dissipates. The beautiful creatures are gone, and I am once again alone.

Leaving Mommy, I turn around and retrace my steps back inside the house. The slate shingles crunch under my slippers, then I bend my knees and slowly shimmy down the slanted roof. Soon I am met with a flat landing that wraps around the entire house. My legs shake, relaxing from the tense moments before bracing myself on the way down.

The gabled window is still open. I kneel, sliding back through it, and immediately I am greeted by a loud banging noise. Daddy. He is locked in my bedroom.

The house echoes with his antics.

Daddy is a doctor for the criminally insane. He has opened asylums across the country, most recently in Sutton, North Carolina.

Daddy encouraged Mommy's fear and is the person that suppressed me.

Together they created someone even more dangerous than the version of me they originally feared.

Cocktails of medication would be placed into a syringe each day and injected into my sleeping body in the middle of the night. There was no routine or schedule to his visits, because no matter how hard I tried to stay awake or predict his next move, I always failed and my eyelids won.

Except for tonight.

The medicine would start wearing off in the evening, and today I took advantage of that. Our old home in the French Quarter has many nooks and crannies, including a dumbwaiter. It was the perfect spot to hide. Shortly after dinner, I raced up to the top story where the platform sat. I crawled inside and curled my tiny frame into it and slid the thick wooden door down. As time passed, my eyes began to get heavy, and I let sleep win.

A commotion woke me. Unsure of how much time had passed, I slowly raised the heavy door and peeked my head out. Mommy was looking back at me.

Her mouth began to open to alert Daddy of my whereabouts, but I stopped her. All I had to do was think about it, and she obeyed.

Next, I squeezed my eyes shut and hoped Daddy was in my room pacing, as he does when frustrated. I demanded the door to close and lock. It slammed, and I jumped. A monstrous roar followed, and I knew my risk was rewarded.

My bedroom window faces the back gardens. I hope he was able to enjoy the masterpiece I performed for him.

My slippers pad against the narrow wood of the attic, and I stomp down the stairs so Daddy can hear that I'm coming, that he's next.

An uncontrollable and chaotic laugh erupts from me, and my vision narrows as shadows surround it. My body skips down the hallway while my fingernails scrape against the wallpaper-covered walls. The brass doorknob at the other end of the hallway twinkles in my eyes. It's all I see. As I reach the door, my body stills, the home quiets, and my eyes flutter closed. A high-pitched scream ends the brief moment of calmness. My eyes shoot open, and the door leaves its hinges and flies against my bedroom wall, shattering on impact. Wooden pieces float, and I'm captivated; they are as sharp as stakes. My eyes shift to the commotion to find Daddy crawling before me, whimpering like a fucking pussy.

Loud screams continue, joined by the flashing of my bedroom light.

Do it.

THE STAKES STAB into him like daggers, going through his legs and into the floor, penetrating his lungs through his back. Blood drips out of his nose and mouth.

"No, son, you don't want to do this," he pleads through wheezing breaths, but his efforts are years too late. In his hand is the syringe. *He* is trying to distract me; *he* thinks I'll show empathy and take mercy, only to allow him to stab me once more, like an obedient dog. Stomping my foot onto the ground, rage fills my body, and heat overwhelms my nerve endings from the tip of my fingers to the ends of my toes.

DING-DONG, can you hear me?
  Do you fear me?
  Kill yourself!

THE SYRINGE LIFTS in his hand, and he jabs himself directly in the jugular, in the primary artery in his neck, which pumps blood to his heart. But he doesn't stop there. Tiny jabs of the needle continue to poke his skin. Long squirts of blood fly out and begin to puddle at his feet. When it comes to the last stab, Daddy pushes the needle through the skin in one fluid downward motion, stopping only once he's reached his collarbone.

His hand falls, and his body follows, landing on the floor with a soft thud; blood bubbles from his lips. He is choking on his own beautiful crimson.

I watch his chest fall and his eyes die, then the light is gone. At the same time the screams stop, the bedroom goes dark, and finally I'm alone.

I'm me.

No moths appear, or maggots. Daddy is not worthy of such beauty.

His name will be defined by this one act. The doctor for the clinically insane, perhaps insane himself?

Stepping over Daddy, I walk to my bed, tired from the night and ready to sleep. But before I am able to, I feel a new energy, one which is not familiar to me.

Spinning around, I'm confused

An older lady in a frumpy brown dress, with white hair and pale skin, appears in the doorway, no emotion visible and no reaction given. Instead, she speaks, and her words come out monotone.

"Prince. You're done now. It's over. This is no longer your home."

2

ROYCE

CURRENT DAY: MID 90S - HOLLOWS
GROVE, PA

I ce.
Chills surround me.

The oval mirror on my vanity frosts before my purple eyes as the tip of my nose turns ice cold. Goosebumps rise on my pale white skin, and my long black nails tap against the gold tabletop as I wait for their next move. A spirit is here.

Agatha Manor has seen life and death, possessions, and sad fucking stories. The house soaks in the energy that was left behind, and I have yet to be any of those things, and all happiness was sucked out of me the moment I arrived all those years ago. The house has never had an opportunity to take anything from me.

Tightness wraps around my bare shoulders. I sit

tall on the upholstered stool, welcoming the embrace in my black silk slip dress. I lean back, but as I do, they leave. The room warms, chills are gone, and the mirror now reveals me, and me alone.

Closing my eyes, I can feel my long lashes tickling my cheeks. "Fuck," hisses out from between my black-painted lips. For once I wish they would just show me who they are, tell me what they want from me, and let me be with them.

I make no effort to hide myself, arms exposed with white ridges. I own my shit.

Softly, I open my eyes, blinking rapidly a few times, then I close my feelings back off one more time. Behind my parted hair of white and black strands stands the man who brings me the most misery, Prince Prescott. His white blond hair and dead eyes look back at me through the mirror. He has two fucking teardrop tattoos under the left eye, bragging about what he did to end up here, while wearing black suit pants and shoes with a white dress shirt open, exposing his bare chest.

I hate him.

What his parents did was horrific, wrong, and inhumane. And he matched that, checkmate, well played, but I still think the teardrop is fucking ridiculous.

"They will never speak to you." His voice is deep and monotone.

Ignoring his tormenting comment, I reach for my perfume bottle that once belonged to my mother, squeeze the pump, and allow the beautiful notes of warm vanilla, orchid, and smoky earth mist over my neck. The scent my mother once wore is no more, because in a fit of rage years ago I smashed the last bottle and immediately regretted it. Since then I have spent sleepless nights and long days trying to replicate it, and this is the closest I've come, but it's still not quite right.

"And it's not *them*." He makes it hurt even more than my brain. I realistically know it can't be; they didn't die here, but a part of me always wishes it could be.

My face remains stone, not feeding into his bait.

Rising from my ottoman, I slip my black tattoo choker on, which completes the outfit, and I am ready to go. My feet padding against the hardwood, I act as if Prince is not standing in my doorway and go to walk past him. His strong hand reaches out, gripping me in the same spot as the choker. Internally, I startle, but externally I give him nothing.

"Take that off," he demands, and I smize, pleased with myself, though I don't respond. My back is slammed against the door, the wind nearly knocked out of me from the force, and Prince squeezes harder now, not allowing me to cough or catch my breath.

With flared nostrils, my foster brother leans closer, and I can feel his warmth. "My hand is the only thing that goes around your neck. You fucking know that." So the story goes, in his own fucking delusions. I stare up at his six-foot-plus frame in defiance, because he doesn't own me.

Prince's lips tickle my ear. "I could do anything I want to you, right now, and you could never stop me." He tries to manipulate me, but I know he can't anymore, and I don't share that information. I'll let him feel like a man with big dick energy if it gets me out of here quicker.

Footsteps echo as they make their way up the stairs, and Prince jumps back, letting me go. Agatha is coming, our housemother. If there is one person he listens to and obeys, it's her. I have yet to be able to figure out why, but that curiosity has never faded.

"You best run off now; don't want your mommy getting mad at you," I taunt in return, knowing he will be unable to retaliate. Prince scoffs, turning on his heel, and storms off down the hall. The walls shake as his door slams; Agatha peeks into my room.

"I'm going to the carnival," I inform her and

brush past her tall frame and plain brown garb. When I say it, I am not looking for permission, as I am of age now and not obligated to tell her anything. I do it out of courtesy. Even if she doesn't deserve it.

"Eventually, darling, you will need to stop being pissed off at the world. They are dead. You are alive. That is your reality and has been for over a decade. Accept it." Smug cunt.

My lungs want to burst with rage and hate, scream until my own eardrums burst, and the mirrors crack. Then push her face into the shards, scarring her face to look like my arms. To have her feel what pain and loss is like and to know the hurt I feel every fucking day.

Instead, I pass her with my chin held high and bite my tongue.

My misery will not be her victory; it will only be mine.

3

ROYCE

1980S - HOLLOWS GROVE, PA

Playing in the front yard of Agatha Manor, alone, I see a shiny black station wagon with tinted windows pull up. My bare feet hit the ground, sliding against the hard earth as I try to stop the swing. It's been sixty-six weeks since I first arrived, and for each day of each week, I have sat upon this swing, from dusk till dawn, trying to manifest *their* return to me.

The roaring engine stops, chirping birds taking over, and the passenger door slowly opens. I watch, glaring toward the small boy who hops out. His hair is bright white, his face is scowled, and his body is stiff; the silk pajamas he is wearing are decorated in dry blood along with his house slippers. The boy's eyes shift, examining his new surroundings. It's obvious he isn't from here from the amount of discomfort radiating from him.

Agatha comes to stand next to him, wearing her classic brown dress. She bends down, whispers in his ear, and his eyes dart forward, focusing on the Manor. It's a two-story square monstrosity, with a dark wooden wraparound porch, black doors, and window trim, a mismatch of tarnished red and white brick siding, and slate roof tiles. Bright green ivy climbs its walls, the only bit of light and joy this place offers, besides the blood-red bathroom, which I have taken a liking to.

An iron fence surrounds the property with a matching gate decorated with beautiful, intricate cobwebs from the peaceful spiders who call it home. A wooden sign with white script staked in the lawn before it says, *Agatha Manor*. On windy nights the unoiled hinges creak, haunting you with the shadows of the tree branches dancing against my bedroom wall.

Agatha Manor is a place where the unusual children are summoned when they have been abandoned or left without parents or guardians. It doesn't matter how the children end up in such predicaments; Agatha senses you are alone with no likelihood of an adult returning, and she comes to fetch you.

It's how I ended up here.

And I wish I wasn't. Since arriving, my body has been numb, and my mind empty with no life left in my eyes.

The manor here in Hollows Grove isn't the only one like it. More exists, but it all depends on who has space for us at the time.

The gate closes and the latch clicks, bringing my attention back to the boy.

Agatha's hand rests on the middle of his back, his body stiff as his brown slip-on house shoes shuffle against the stone walkway. Mechanically his knees rise with each step up the porch, and not once does he look over to me. Wandering eyes are startled by his hand; an XO with a deranged smile tattoo is inked on it. I hold in my shock, keeping my face unbothered.

Because, like me, he is now dead inside too.

THE SUN HAS LONG since set; the loud cowbell has called me to dinner, but on my swing is where I remain still. I have not seen the boy again.

"Royce, bath and bed. Now!" Agatha's one-cigarette-too-many voice punctures my ears. Looking over, I see her head sticking out of her bedroom window. My eyes roll, which thankfully she doesn't catch, as I hop off the swing and rush inside.

I learned after the first time to never play with her because she doesn't find the antics of children funny. She pulled me out of the bath, naked and dripping with water, to deliver ten of the most painful lashings on my bottom. Each one stung more than the last, and every time I winced, she would hit me harder; the crack of the leather against my skin would get louder. Many lessons were learned.

Dim lights greet me as I walk inside; the floorboards creak under my feet as I race up the stairs, taking two at a time. Since I missed dinner, I must wait until tomorrow's breakfast to eat, something that doesn't faze me, as I haven't been hungry in sixty-six weeks.

Reaching the top, I turn toward my bathroom when I'm startled, my body crashing into *his*, but he doesn't move, completely unaffected.

Stumbling backward, I catch my balance before falling.

"Why is your hair like that?" his prepubescent voice says.

My face contorts, confused by his question, before responding in a hushed whisper, "Because I was born this way?"

Shrugging his shoulders, he seems satisfied with my response.

I watch his eyes, trying to take a read on him. The boy blinks, and his irises turn white momentarily before returning to their natural brown state. At the same time, I hear soft whispers behind me. Agatha. He looks up, focusing on Agatha, and walks past me, heading toward her.

"Royce, this is Prince, our new guest."

I don't turn around or acknowledge her words. The air seems uneasy, and all I want to do is escape it.

Building up courage, my bare feet move, and I rush to the bathroom. She doesn't stop me, and my shoulders slump in relief. As I reach my destination, I flick on the light and hurry to close the thick wooden door behind me.

Red tiles welcome me, from the floor to the walls and ceiling. The countertop is black with matching cabinets and fixtures. Frosted glass lanterns hang from the wall, and as I turn to face the mirror, which is framed in black, my purple eyes look back at me, and the corner of my lip hitches, just like my mom's. And my hair, which is perfectly parted down the middle, is a combination of both my moms, half black and the other half white.

I'm always reminded of them; there is no escaping it. And I fucking hate it!

Screaming, my fist clenches, and my knuckles connect with the cold glass.

It cracks, shattering into multiple jagged shards and falling around me. With a heavy breath, I reach for one and make the first cut of the day. This one is farther above my exposed arm, on untouched skin. Pushing the sharp end into my flesh and sliding it slowly, one end to the other, droplets of blood follow, running down my pale skin. I smile, bringing my tongue to it, and lick the crimson. Its metallic flavor erupts on my taste buds, and my eyes close in sweet ecstasy.

This is what it feels like to live.

4

ROYCE

1980S - HOLLOWS GROVE, PA

The sun has risen twice since the last time I saw Prince.

At first, I was unbothered. It was another day just like the last, spent alone. But then, as it does, my mind wandered and became curious.

Today, I have decided to find the boy.

Opening my bedroom door, I peer out, and it seems that I am alone. Down the hall, where a door once remained open, day in and day out, it is now closed; it has to be his room.

On my tiptoes, I creep down the hallway. Just like the exterior, the inside is just as darkly decorated. Wall sconces hang, shining a dim yellow light; the windows are tinted, not allowing sunlight to invade, and old pictures of people I've never seen before decorate the walls.

Passing the stairs, I am almost there when a floorboard squeaks below me. I pause, my mind racing, and I decide to walk loudly toward the stairs as if I am going down them to resume my position outside on the tree swing.

With hopes my act of deception works, my body stands frozen at the stair opening; I wait to ensure no one comes to check on the curious noises in the hall. Time passes slowly, but patience is important. No one comes, no one cares, and I continue my mission.

Nervously, I inhale through my nose; I tiptoe farther down the hall, staying close to the wall in an effort to avoid any other unpredictable squeaky floorboards. Reaching the door, my eyes shift to the right, where a narrow hallway continues to Agatha's suite. Her door is always closed, and I dare never sneak into it. I truly believe she would kill me if I tried.

Placing my ear against the cool wood, it sends a chill down my body, and my hairs rise. It's the middle of summer; this doesn't make sense. The door is ice, like all the happiness in the world was sucked out of the air, leaving only sadness and empty souls behind. My curiosity piques even more.

Who is this boy? The blood on his pajamas, the white eyes, his strange question. I need to know more.

Bringing my hand to the black iron doorknob, I find it's freezing, and my skin sticks to it instantly like a warm tongue to a frozen pole in the winter.

I swallow and start turning it, millimeter by millimeter.

My teeth try to chatter, but I stick my tongue between them to stop any noise. I keep at this for nearly two minutes, slow and steady. As I feel the knob give less resistance, I know I have made it all the way, and it is now time to push the door open.

Every part of me is hoping the old hinges don't expose me.

A sliver of light greets the darkness of the hall-way. His bed is against the wall within my view, and Prince is levitating. My brow furrows.

What the fuck?

Soft whispers are being spoken. It's Agatha.

"Vanquish the demons. Vanquish the thoughts. Deprive yourself of all sensations. Or forgive you, I will not."

Opening the door ever so slightly more, I find Agatha's hands are trembling as her palms face him, and she repeats herself once more. "Vanquish the demons. Vanquish the thoughts. Deprive yourself of all sensations. Or forgive you, I will not."

The second time hits harder. My body reacts as if it's heard this spell before. Closing my eyes, I search my memory far and wide but come up dry. Reaching my free hand to my hair, I scrunch it, then pull at the strands out of frustration. Where have I heard this? Why is it so triggering?

My hand lets go of the cold iron knob, and my fingernails begin to tap against it, and it's as soon as I start that I know I have majorly fucked up.

The door swings open fully, anger and aggression following, and the bedroom light explodes just as Prince's body falls hard against the mattress.

Agatha shouts with the most intensity I've ever experienced, "Out, child! OUT!" The wall sconces flicker, the house falls dark, and I am fucking terrified.

Peeling my face off the door, my body stumbles backward, and my bare feet trip on the dark hallway rug before rushing back to my bedroom. My chest heaves, anxiety coursing through me. And I know only bad things will come of this. I slam the door behind me, hoping to buy another second of time before the fury kicks up.

Footsteps stomp down the hall, and they become

louder and louder the closer they get. I scurry to my bed and jump on top of it. It's unmade, and I huddle my legs under the sheets, bringing my knees to my chest, and wait. The door swings open, and Agatha stands at the threshold with her arms crossed, a scowl on her face, and her words are spoken slowly when she says, "Don't you dare open a closed door in this house again. You know the rules. Or were they not clear enough for you?"

My head nods rapidly, terrified of what's to come. I am not getting out of this easily.

Stepping forward, her arms uncross. My eyes water, and my lip attempts to quiver.

Taking three large steps, Agatha reaches me, and her hand cups my face, squeezing it tightly in her grip. It hurts. She could crush my skull if she wanted to, but I won't let a tear fall in her presence; I will leave this earth with the little dignity I have left. With all the willpower I can muster up, I hold it in.

My mind dissociates, familiar voices enter my head, reminding me how strong I am, and I hold on to that for as long as I can, which isn't long at all because Agatha breaks the silence and reminds me of my worth.

"Did you learn nothing from your moms' death?"

Her words sting like venom.

My moms were master witches in Hollows Grove and taught at the local university. Until that day sixty-six weeks ago, when I rushed into their home lab, interrupting one of the million experiments they would conduct. I needed to show them the cool trick my familiar could do, but it has now become my biggest regret. The spell was broken, potions smashed, and they immediately perished, first turning to stone, then to dust.

Ashes to ashes, dust to dust.

My familiar scurried away immediately, then Agatha appeared and my powers vanished.

"I'd discipline you, but it looks like you are capable of that yourself." Her eyes shift to my exposed arm before pushing my head back against the pillow.

I don't blink. I don't cry.

Moving my eyes off her, I focus on the once-empty doorway Prince is now occupying, wearing black pants and a white button-up. A smug look is etched on his face, and it's in this moment I know I'm fucked.

He will never be an ally, only my enemy.

5

ROYCE

CURRENT DAY: 1990S - HOLLOWS GROVE, PA

The day is done, and the night is dark.

My feet crunch on top of dried fall leaves clustered on the old dirt path through the woods.

The air is chilled, but I don't wear a cardigan. As someone who hates feeling, this is how I torture myself, by feeling everything.

I feel *him*, his eyes and presence. *He* is always lurking.

It started years ago, the fascination, the fixation. No efforts are ever made to hide it, as Prince has no shame and respects no boundaries. A feeling that once brought me extreme anxiety and stress now leaves me feeling exhausted. *He* isn't hurting me; if that's his goal, I hurt myself enough every fucking day for the both of us.

Long strides bring me to an all-too-familiar place, my bare leg exposed through the slit in my thin silk nightdress, and goosebumps form as I get closer.

I deserve everything I put myself through.

Because I killed them.

They should be here, living freely at my childhood home.

It's an old log cabin surrounded by beautiful, lush trees; in the spring and summer it's the most beautiful spot in all of Hollows Grove, as that's when our home would truly blossom. I would play in the large garden where they would grow and collect flowers and herbs for their projects; they built our home when they found out I was coming.

And now, as I stand before it, its life is gone. The wood is rotten, windows smashed in, and the garden is overgrown and dead. I walk to the front door, gently pushing it open. As I do, the hinges creak, followed by owls hooting. It spooks me, and my breath hitches as I continue to step inside.

The smells that once comforted me are gone, the eclectic decor is now rotted, and parts of the floor caved in from the explosion in their lab below.

A heel clicks behind me, but I don't turn.

It's Prince.

Ignoring him, I step closer to the gaping hole. I peer down, then squeeze my eyes shut. Everything floods back to me, even the smells from that day, including the smoke.

A scream erupts from my throat, and my body feels like I am being sucked backward, with images of days and years from the past flying swiftly by.

Then it stops, the screaming, the moving, and my body sways as I find my balance.

As I open my eyes, they shift slowly, and I am no longer looking down through the floor. My head tilts up and the hole is closed. A stark white ceiling looks back at me with bright fluorescent lighting.

It's all so sterile, the tile floor cold against my bare feet.

A smashing of glass catches my attention, and my head jolts toward the sound.

Trembling fingers cover my mouth as a gasp exits. My moms are here.

They are just as they were on that fateful day, perfectly beautiful and captivated by their craft. Both are wearing black lab coats. Mom is barefoot like me, with her toes sticking out from under her long black dress. Mommy is wearing lounge pants and a tee, and she is giggling at something Mom must have said.

Looking down, the vial that smashed to the ground appears to be empty. A wave of relief strikes me.

"Darling, should we try for another? Give Royce a friend to play with?" Mom asks, looking up adoringly at Mommy.

She is quick to reply. "Absolutely."

My shock transforms to grief for the sibling who never was.

They stay silent, looking at one another as two true soulmates would. Their love could fill a room with a single look, just as it is now.

I'm jolted forward, my breath taken from me as life speeds by; time is fast-forwarding.

Nausea ripples through me, and just as I think I am going to get sick, it all abruptly stops. My heart races as my eyes adjust and my body shakes. The room is unchanged, but my moms are now in the middle of an experiment, and my heart immediately sinks into my stomach.

With plastic safety goggles covering their eyes, Mom is bent over, her long black hair hanging over her shoulders as she steadily clamps a glass flask with purple liquid bubbling inside. Mommy is whispering a mantra repetitively with her hands over it. Her voice becomes more commanding with each word, and I watch eagerly in anticipation. What are they brewing?

As I wait for it to be revealed, tiny footsteps echo in my ear. They are getting closer and closer. My eyes move to the stairs, and a little girl with half white and black hair hops off the bottom step with excitement nearly bursting out of her. Following behind is her familiar, my familiar.

My head turns, and dread creeps up my body. I've seen this story before.

The pads of my feet against the tile break my moms' concentration, and the spell is interrupted as mom's hand loses its grip on the tongs that are holding the flask, and in slow motion it falls to the ground.

No, no, no.

I am being forced to watch my younger self watch my parents die.

Purple flames take over, flickering violently and engulfing my moms. As quickly as it appeared, it evaporates as if it were never here at all, and calmness enters.

Squinting my eyes out of confusion, I see both of my moms are frozen still. *Why aren't they moving?*

Looking over to my younger self, I see her screaming, and she is fucking scared.

My body tries to move. I want to protect her from what's to come, but I am stuck in place.

No, no, no.

A faded voice, one I don't recognize, enters the room. A slight wind follows, and my brow wrinkles in confusion. I don't remember this.

"And your time here is done," is whispered, and all the air feels like it is being sucked out of the room as I watch them turn to ashes, then dust floating away one more time.

Time fast-forwards; my body travels through the many vortexes and lives, bringing me back to the present and standing before the open floor, looking down.

"What did you do?" I shout, unable to move.

His heels click once more behind me. A deep voice murmurs, "Nothing."

And I believe him. He would never lie about torturing a soul. It's been his primary objective since arriving in my life all those years ago, because he openly tortures mine daily and fucking loves it.

Their headstones stand in the graveyard, but no remains lie under the earth. Their ashes blew away, leaving me with only memories and regret, with the tiniest bit of hope that my moms will one day visit me.

Was this *them?* After all the years I have come here, why now?

Lost in thought, I don't even realize Prince has gotten closer to me until I feel his breath dancing across my bare shoulder as he speaks. "*They* broke you for me; I should thank them." His hand covers my mouth. It's his hand with the scratchy mouth tattoo and XO eyes.

I don't tremble or panic. This is something I am all too familiar with, sadly.

Fighting only gets him harder.

He's lost his power. It happened after he killed his parents all those years ago, so this is the only power he can claim to have, but power is not what I give him.

Prince has been doing this since I turned of age. He is a year older than me. Perhaps he also wishes to be commended for such restraint, waiting for as long as he did, but those words of praise will never leave my lips. What he does is vile, and his reasons are invalid. He isn't a man; he is a coward.

As a teen, I caught him many times peering in when I was relaxing in the bath or looking too deeply into my eyes. Lurking in the shadows if I was to go out, threatening anyone who dared to look at me for too long.

In his mind, this behavior is acceptable. It's not.

His hips grind against me, and his cock hardens. "Forever mine, sweet, beautiful girl."

I will never be his. But I grind my hips in return against him. Prince likes the fight, and I will never give him the satisfaction.

His soft, strong hand inches its way down my chin and around my neck. He squeezes, then hisses as I lean farther into him.

Next, I hear his belt unbuckle, and the unzipping of his trousers follows. His hips shimmy against my body, encouraging his trousers to fall and bunch around his feet.

At the same time, slowly, the delicate silk of my dress slides up my legs and over my backside. Prince holds it tightly, gathered at my hips. I don't have panties on, leaving me exposed before him, vulnerable, just how he likes me.

The tip of his hard cock bobs against my skin. I feel the precum leaking from his tip before I bend over slightly, preparing for his intrusion.

There is no point in trying to stop him.

Prince pulls me tight against him, angling my hips higher and leaving me on tiptoes.

Looking down, my heart drops, and adrenaline

kicks in. All it would take is his release, and I would be falling headfirst into my own demise.

What an ironic turn of events that would be.

My neck is freed, but his phantom touch stays as he lines himself up with my pussy.

He is not one to play with a meal before devouring it whole.

The vile sound of that man spitting, not once but twice, onto his cock sends chills up my spine. Prince wastes no time, forcibly thrusting into me. His movements are rough as his pelvis slaps against my bare ass. My pussy reacts, and I grip him instantly while my breath hitches.

Something I learned years ago is that I may as well make the most out of it and use him in return.

"Sweet girl, you always feel so fucking good," he praises with his raspy voice. Both hands are now holding my hips, holding me still while he fucks me mercifully, dominating me.

His movements are hurried as he has one goal in mind: mark me, claim me, own me.

Loud grunts echo around us, and my own moans follow. Bringing my fingers to my clit, working myself and adding to my insatiable need to come.

I love coming. I love fucking. My preference is to

fuck myself, but a helping cock will never be denied. But I hate that it's *his* cock.

A part of me is convinced Prince also knows this, that he's watched me before while I am alone in my room in the middle of the night. But I have never caught him. And now he can bring his vile fantasies to life. How he lurks in the dark, stalking me, prowling, then pouncing just as a predator would his prey in the wild.

Thrusting into me harder, his cock hits all the right places, damn him. My mind and body battle, but my body always wins.

My toes scrunch, sliding against the hardwood as the all-too-familiar tingling sensation builds.

With my thumb and forefinger, I squeeze my sensitive nub. Fuck, I am addicted.

I will always be an addict to this feeling.

Jolts of electricity flow freely through my limbs, and each breath taken has turned into panting breaths. The walls of my cunt grip him harder, and my orgasm ripples through me, causing my body to tremble, giving in to the sweet release.

It's almost immediate; his cum begins to fill me, and his movements slow, relishing his victory.

Hair is falling around my face, some sticking to the beads of sweat that have decorated my skin. It doesn't bother me as I rub my clit a few more times, milking every inch of this orgasm and his cock, taking everything I can from them both.

Prince purrs, "I fucking hate you. I will always destroy you because you are mine." The muscles in my chest clench, refusing to let me feel the impact of his words, just before he pulls out of me.

I am not a possession. He does not own me. I simply tolerate him.

Breathlessly, I rise, not responding. My dress shimmies slowly back down my body, covering up what was just on display to him. It doesn't take long for me to feel our cum dripping down my inner thighs, and I do nothing to stop it. Instead, I spin around on the tips of my toes and look into his dark eyes. Teardrop tattoos stare back at me. White hair hangs, disheveled-looking, over his pale forehead. Leaning forward, I place my hand onto his exposed bare chest, compliments of his unbuttoned dress shirt.

This is how he always dresses. Smart trousers and undone shirts paired with dress shoes. Sometimes he honors us with a suit vest.

Prince is one of the most pretentious twats I have ever met.

Leaning forward, our lips are only millimeters apart. His face is flushed, and his nostrils flare.

Grinding my pussy against his cock, he is aroused once more, and I couldn't care less as I smirk to myself.

Whispering, I remind him where he stands with me, "Lock up when you're done," adding a cheeky wink before skipping past him.

An audible sigh follows when my back is turned, but I am unable to see his annoyance with me. How unfortunate.

Leaving my childhood home, memories remain of this evening, but I feel nothing.

He has managed to kill me once more.

6

PRINCE

Royce walks through the woods, my cum dripping from her cunt. With the cool night's temperature, I know it's already starting to dry on her inner thigh. The permanency of it fills me with overwhelming satisfaction.

I've hated her since the moment I arrived in this forsaken place. My abilities disappeared, and resentment overflowed. As the years passed, anger and loathing turned into a game with her, and I regret nothing and feel no remorse. I'll forever be her hunter, and she, my prey.

My displeasure doesn't solely fall upon Royce; Agatha also collects a share of it, but I do not crave to taste Agatha as I do Royce. That old bitch lives because I allow it and will continue to live until I allow it no more.

Brushing my hair off my forehead, my eyes still following my sweet Royce, bright colorful lights bounce through the large, bare hanging tree limbs. Then something unusual happens; my sweet girl adds a skip and a hop to her step as her ever-so-unique hair sashays back and forth across her long, lean back.

Why is she happy?

The Fright Night Carnival graces our town each year with grungy yellow-and-red tents that have dulled over time. Rides that make small children violently vomit afterward or jump with horrific glee. Sideshows are a given. Our entire town of Hollows Grove is a fucking sideshow, for crying out loud. Yet the crowds gather to have one night of fake thrills.

Perhaps one day I will give this place a thrill worth remembering. Until then, I digress.

Reaching the edge of the forest, my eyes continue to watch Royce. Her feet skip with more speed as she races down the long, grassy hill.

Before following suit, I peer up. Looking from far above our town, off in the distance, I spot Trick or Treat, the local strip joint. The sign shines in bright neon pink against dark wood, showcasing one of its many talented witches who work there. But for a brief moment, my mind wanders. Ditching my sweet girl for instant gratification would be less of a hassle; however, I crave the chase too much. I feel my cock twitch against my trousers. To not hunt *her* would only send me spiraling and spinning.

Sweeping my eyes back toward Fright Night, Royce's silhouette frolics farther away from me. My feet move, on instinct, with no thought. The smell of her fragrance lingers in the air, warm vanilla with seductive oud, a sensual earthy note, and I follow, knowing it will lead me to her.

Dry grass crunches beneath my shoes, the slant of the hill propelling me forward. My gaze moves down, watching my movements to ensure I don't fall or trip over myself and make a fucking scene. As I reach the bottom, mesh fencing greets me, trapping everyone inside. I smirk. Oh, what a sight to be seen.

The vision of screaming crowds and roaring fires greets me. Blinking once removes it from my fore-thought; it's only torture when I realize I cannot act upon it.

Following the fence line, my fingertips touch the cool metal, sliding against it as I walk. The sight of witches, goblins, fairies, and ghosts, both families and couples on dates, appears as I turn around the corner to be greeted by the entrance. Two black booths block the opening, and an orange crossbar rises with each payment to the cashiers, who are skeletons with name tags. Luke and Yeti. Neither have eyeballs; how they got this job is perplexing, but nonetheless, their system seems to be working. Stepping up, I hand Yeti a twenty from my wallet. The orange bar rises, and he, I assume, waves me through. "Make it out by midnight, or you'll never escape." Raising my brows at the ominous statement, I nod and walk through.

The sound of classic carnival music greets me, the smell of fried shitty food lingers, and the sideshow freaks mingle, attempting to draw people into their booths and tents.

Some have chaotic pink, purple, and green hair, pale skin with cool-tone death makeup, long nails, and scantily clad garments hiding their pelvis regions with black tape forming X's covering their perky nipples. One walks over to me, his stiletto nail scratching under my chin and causing my head to turn. His eyes are seductive, and as he narrows his lips, white smoke faintly dances from his breath. The aroma is alluring, my eyes hood and my heartbeat can be heard in my ears. Biting my lip, I inch forward, sucking it in. It electrifies my body. Placing my hands on his strong chest and my cock grinding against his, I whisper breathlessly, "Later, I'll come back for you."

This mysterious man breaks the connection first, stepping back and releasing me from his captivity. My eyes blink as I come out of his spell. Confused, I step back, questioning, "What was that?" Genuinely intrigued, as I have never experienced a spell such as this before.

He tsks me. "If I told you it wouldn't be fun anymore, would it?" The seductress is right; the unknown is half the allure. Pondering his words, I nod, accepting it for now, and turn away.

A small breeze follows, allowing me to catch her scent once more. Closing my eyes, my body pivots, following it. Before I disappear from the main drag, my head turns, looking back briefly as my eyes open. What a fucking delicious specimen to devour later.

With hurried feet, I continue on my mission, Royce. It pleases me to know anyone capable of sniffing out scents will stay far away from her because I mark what's mine. But not all will be able to tell, leading us to now, and why I follow.

The crowds thin out the deeper down the side

path I go. Old witches' cackling echoes, and the lights dim. Creatures linger in the shadows, only revealing themselves as I pass by.

Why would she come here?

It isn't long before I catch up. Stopping in my tracks, I am taken aback by the sight before me.

She isn't alone.

Her long fingers are intertwined with *his*.

Her free hand reaches over, holding on to his forearm as her head leans against his bicep.

His tattoos shine, made of silver glimmer, decorating every inch of exposed, nearly see-through, pale skin I can see.

Contrary to popular belief, vampires do not turn to dust under the sun. They shine bright like a million tiny diamonds. Some, like this fucker, get intricate designs done on their skin, making their glimmer more unique. As the dim light catches the artwork, it shines similarly to when they are in the sun.

Wearing blue distressed jeans, sneakers, a tee, and chipped black nail polish, his head turns to look upon *her*, smiling.

How dare he!

My blood boils. Red fills my vision as I inject him

with poisonous blood, destroying his plasma. Loud, deep screams fill my ears, and his teeth chatter so hard his sharp fangs fracture. The sizzling of skin follows, and the poison burns right through it, making his death a painful one. Lastly, before it's all over, I command him to take the cross I freshly sharpened and stab it into his heart. He does, ever so obediently.

Rightfully deserved.

Then, one blink is all it takes, and my vision vanishes. Revealing to me that the reality of my situation is still unfortunate.

I wish the blasted curse away from me. My fists clench out of frustration. Returning my focus ahead, I catch a glimpse of Royce's hair disappearing into a tent.

Curious, indeed.

Standing outside of the slit in the fabric, I peer around, looking for any indication of what tent this could be, with nothing to be found. Fingertips dance against the scratchy fabric before reaching between the slit. Pulling it back, ever so slightly, my eyes peer through the narrow gap I've created. The area empty; only brown earth layers the ground with long, thick ropes hanging from the intricate trapeze system. This tent only has a couple of rows of benches and is adequate but incredibly smaller than the other venue for such a performance here.

Faint giggles keep me moving.

The gentle waving of thin fabric intrigues me, guiding me toward it.

Peering through, it's a small space with a couple mirrors and wooden costume chests. Stepping in, my eyes continue to wander around the tight space until I find her.

Her backside is leaning against a small table with her head thrown back, the ends of her hair falling on top of it while both hands grip the edge. *He* is devouring her mouth. His fingers linger up the slit of her cool silk slip dress, brushing against her thigh. Royce doesn't stop him.

A moan escapes her as his fingers impale her throbbing pussy.

There's nothing she loves more than an orgasm.

Blood boiling, it takes every inch of willpower I have for me to not interject and kill him now. I'd thrive in a carnival bloodbath. Then my sweet girl's purple eyes squint, feeling my presence as she peeks over to me. They widen immediately, fear vibrating off her as *he* continues to fingerbang her. Placing my index finger before my lips, I indicate she must keep quiet and turn away. Because I love playing the game, taunting and stalking my prey before we play.

Clasping my hands together as I leave the tent, excitement riddles through me. Satisfaction follows, because it's my cum inside of her that is coating his fingers, not hers.

Royce may have her fun tonight. But tomorrow, they will both reel from the consequences.

7

ROYCE

S hit.

Closing my eyes, they water, but never do I let a tear fall.

Beckham mustn't know I am upset. He is the only one I care about and have vowed to love and protect until the end of our time. Beckham Black-heart has been mine to keep for nearly two years. And no one has known... until now.

Taking a deep breath through my nose, I allow myself to fall back into the moment of pure, unapologetic happiness I was experiencing before feeling *his* presence among us. Beckham has heard tales of my foster brother, Prince, but I have never elaborated on the extent of it all. The battle would be full of bloodshed and heartache, not one I think I could withstand if I lost this man. Prince would fucking destroy him, and I say that because it's true. Beckham is fiercely protective, but Prince, he never stops. The level of pure hatred coursing through his veins is something I strongly believe no one could stand up to and survive.

And now, Prince knows about him. He could take what's mine away from me in the blink of an eye. My heart drops into the pit of my stomach.

Shaking my head ever so slightly, ridding my mind of the possibilities and returning to the present, I give in to Beckham's touch, allowing the ecstasy of being with him, my mate, to take over. Beckham lowers his tight jeans, allowing them to bunch at his ankles, while I adjust myself. Sitting on top of the small desk, legs spread, my dripping pussy is on display with my dress gathered at my hips.

The palm of his hand rubs against me, and my hips grind against his soft skin, my clit craving him.

"She's mine. You. Are. Mine." His declaration of ownership over me fills my body with warmth and need. Leaning forward, my lips brush against his jawline and my breath dances along his skin. "And you are mine," Beckham growls, then hisses, "fucking forever. I belong to you."

At the same time as he speaks his promise, I feel

his hand move, and it is replaced by his hard cock slamming into me.

A loud moan releases from me as I accept every fucking inch of him. Desperately, I need his cum to replace what is currently inside of me. I can't stand having Prince inside me for a moment longer. Wrapping my legs around his narrow waist, I need him closer to me. It's never enough; I will always crave more.

Our lips lock, and it feels as if we are sucking each other's souls, the energy that passes through us sending shivers down my spine as goosebumps form along my skin. Squeezing my bare heels against his bare ass, I pull him closer, using him, grinding my clit against his pelvis. My walls grip him as his movements become more hurried. The mixture of moans and panting through my nose becomes more audible in the small space and sweat beads along my forehead. Squeezing the desk with my fingers, the sensation we are both chasing starts to build.

Beckham breaks the kiss, his lashes brushing against mine, followed by his strong hands gripping my face. Warm breath tickles me as I open my eyes to meet his beautiful amber stare.

My orgasm builds in my lower abdomen, and with a quivering lip and flexed toes, I give in. And

Beckham is quick to follow. Ropes of his warm cum coat me. "Fuck, baby, you feel so good." My words are soft and husky; meanwhile, his are spoken with a tremble. "You are my home." And my heart instantly melts; I love this man.

Lost in the moment, our focus is solely on each other because nothing else in the world matters right now. Being this consumed by one another could be detrimental, because Prince is surely still lurking around, waiting and plotting. But before I allow those thoughts to run rampant, the old wooden table gives out, and we go down with it.

Beckham and I both look at each other in shock. What in the actual fuck just happened? A cloud of dust floats around us, and the shock quickly turns into loud laughter. His cock is still inside of me as I clenched my walls tighter to keep it safe as we went down. And his hands are no longer on my face; they are instead on either side of me as he braces us for landing.

Burying my face into the crook of his neck, I breathe in his scent in an effort to muffle my hysterics.

"Baby, only with you would this happen." Beckham chuckles into my hair. The tip of my tongue sticks out, tracing the indentations and ridges along his skin, and my sharp nails scratch his back. The memory of how it happened flashes in front of me.

It was instant; one look, and we saw each other, I mean, really fucking saw each other. Our hearts and souls connected, and we had to have one another. We didn't act on it then, but days passed, cravings increased, while my body ached, desperate to be around him again.

I couldn't take it any longer; then five days passed since seeing him in the woods. Five days of me cowering in my room, trying to fight the inevitable.

The house is quiet; the sun has fallen while I lay with sweaty palms in my bed. With each tick of the clock my anxiety rises, but it has to be tonight. With one swift move, my body shoots up, sliding my second-story bedroom window open and closing my eyes. I jump.

The silk of my white dress flutters, and the fall feels like minutes, not seconds, before I finally land on both feet. It stings, sending a shock up my bones, causing me to fall over. My hands braced for it, hitting the earth at the same time to not further injure myself. I lie like this for minutes, waiting for the tingling to subside. The night is calm; no movement from inside the house could be heard; I'm almost there. The plan is nearly complete.

Steadily, I begin to lift myself up, taking a deep breath in and brushing the dirt off of me.

Standing still, my eyes shift one last time before my feet take off running into the thick tree line. A giant smile adorns my face. I fucking did it. Once in the shadows of the forest, I stop to catch my breath and hope this was all worth it. Please be there.

Hours pass, and the beds of my feet are tattered from pebbles and branches. Any noise and my body stops, hoping it's him. But it never is.

Feeling defeated, my back slides down a large trunk. The bark scratches me, but it's fine. Any marks I can explain due to my tendency to be reckless.

Resting my head, it falls back, then a male's voice can be heard. "Don't be sad, baby. I'm sorry I'm so late."

Nervous, I bring my knees into myself, wrapping my arms around them. Looking around, I don't see anyone. A couple of owls hoot, bringing my attention to the night sky, which is decorated with bright stars. They are so beautiful, I could get lost in them forever.

My concentration is broken when the crack of a branch next to me puts me on alert. Looking back down, what is mine stands before me. He is casual and so fucking cool, his hands in his pant pockets, combat boots on his feet and crossed at the ankles as he leans against a tree across from me. In a black tee with black hair and the cockiest grin on his face, I smile.

His hand reaches out, and without a thought, I take it as he helps me rise. It's electric.

Looking up at him and his over-six-foot frame to my barely five-foot-one, I make the first move, gripping his face and planting my lips on his.

He hisses, like it stings, but it doesn't stop me. Our tongues meet, dancing, battling for dominance, and I give in, allowing him to take control. His hands grip my waist, and my legs wrap around him.

"I need you inside of me," I whisper against his lips, and he wastes no time undoing his pants and sliding into my soaked pussy. We fuck like rabid animals, our movements quick and hard. Neither one of us will last long. Then, just before I come, something out of the ordinary happens. I have a distinct urge to mark him, claim him. To make him fucking mine.

Saliva builds in my mouth, the craving increasing with each passing moment since this thought enters my mind. Bringing my lips to his cool, soft neck, I bite down, deep without hesitation. My teeth sink in and break his thin, delicate skin as my body quivers, releasing all over his cock.

His movements become more feral, and his hard cock pounds into my pussy relentlessly, neither of us refusing to let up. And instead of a metal taste erupting on my taste buds, it's more salty, which confuses me. His instinct is quick as his senses react, and with a sensual moan into my ear, he whispers, "I'm a vampire, baby. It's not blood; it's fucking magic."

Meaning, blood doesn't freely flow through him. They drink it to survive but don't produce it. Regardless, it's my new favorite addiction.

My teeth release from him as I feel him filling me up, coating my pussy with his cum. At the same time, he begins to lower us to the ground, laying me gently on my back. Pulling out, cum is still shooting out of his cock, landing on my inner thighs as we watch it drip down.

Lowering his head between my legs, he glances up at me, his eyes dark and his smile large with sharp teeth exposed. His eyes never leaving mine, his head continues to move slowly while his lips trace along my exposed skin, teasing me. Goosebumps riddle me as my stomach knots in anticipation. As this beautiful fucking man nips at my flesh, the moonlight catches his canines, allowing them to glisten before they become embedded in my skin.

I'm aroused. Something he can sense as his warm tongue teases my skin. A moan of his own follows, and his eyes roll into the back of his head.

My pussy throbs, needing more while my back arches. His thick, dark hair is too good to resist, so I entangle my fingers through it, encouraging him to never stop as my body vibrates in desire.

"Mine," I declare, and his eyes look up at me and wink. A mixture of blood and cum runs down his chin, and I know I am keeping him for the rest of my life.

He breaks away from the bite, and I take my fingers from his hair and swipe my thumb along his chin. I want to taste it too.

Slipping my thumb between my swollen lips, I suck back his release mixed with my savory blood, a moan slipping as my soul begs for more of our sweet nectar.

"Beckham." He shyly introduces himself with hooded eyes filled with lust.

And I share my name in return. "Royce."

From that night on, there has been no one else. Beckham has my heart and soul, just as I have his. And Prince doesn't count.

Makeup hides Beckham's mark, our bond, our eternity together. I will and have done anything and everything to keep him safe. Lying, cheating, and sweet deception included. My foster brother had no idea I was doing so fucking good until now.

Now, fear ripples through my bones, not for me, because I can take whatever he delivers, but for what's mine, Beckham.

I try to shake all negative thoughts from the forefront of my brain.

Prince is impulsive and obsessive, but he's not

stupid. Anything that may happen won't be done until he gets me alone.

Glancing, lines to rides build, and as we walk past them, I'm not sure how much time has passed, but we are back on the main cobbled path of Fright Night.

Beckham leans over, softly whispering against my bare shoulder, "I was wondering when you were going to come back to me."

I smile. "I was just thinking about when we first met."

My words encourage his smile to grow. "I love you, baby." His lips pepper kisses on my skin, and I melt.

"Royce!" A deep voice startles me, and I jump. Looking next to me, with my hand on my chest, I see it's just Jerry.

Jerry is our town's plumber; the guy knows his pipes. It's important to note he is also a fairy, or fae, so I'm sure having magic helps with his customer satisfaction. With small pink wings, a faded white crop top, and black acid-washed shorts showing off his curvy, tattooed frame, he flutters next to us.

"Let Agatha know I will stop by tomorrow; the part we were waiting for has arrived." His excitement for the trade is fascinating and nearly contagious.

I reply, "Absolutely, Jerry."

Scratching his bald head, he kicks his distressed work boot-clad feet and flies away.

"The guy is a legend, I'm telling you." Beckham treats Jerry like he's a hero. Always have. Like I said, it's nearly contagious, just not to me.

8

ROYCE

The ride is fast, causing my hair to hang toward the earth, which feels miles away. I am free. The only restraints are the ones crossing over my chest. Adrenaline is how I feel alive in my suppressed world. Each deep breath welcomes fresh air to my lungs, and as the ride spins, the breeze flutters against my skin. I am happy.

Raising my arms, the ride circles around once more, and my body releases a therapeutic scream. Embracing it, I squeeze my eyes shut and give it all I fucking have. Passing the bottom, my body is upright, and my hair falls over my face but doesn't stop me. Thankfully, straps cross over my waist, ensuring the children and elders don't get a full view of my coochie, compliments of my dress.

On the last spin, I relax into the bodyboard and just be for five more seconds. The seconds pass swiftly as the ride comes to a stop. It's my turn to jump off. The carnival worker unbuckles me, and I hop onto the platform. His eyes are looking me over, more specifically my arms. The scars.

Pointing to my largest cut with a ridged scar that most definitely could have used stitches, I toy with him. "I used hedge trimmers, nearly lost my arm." He's startled from my casual statement. But I feel no shame. It's him who should feel embarrassment. His lips move, an apology about to follow suit, but I have no interest in hearing it and instead walk away, silently.

The guy is a goblin, and he should really be the last person to judge, but they are known for being pretentious assholes, just like Prince.

Beckham is waiting for me off to the side. It takes a moment for my eyes to find him, and when I do, my lips stretch in a smile while my eyes take him in. Biting my lip, I skip over to his strong body that's leaning against the railing. His arms wrap around my delicate frame while my face tucks into the crook of his neck. Inhaling deeply, Beckham's scent overwhelms me with familiarity and happiness, musk and wood. Lips kiss the crown of my head, and I ease into him fully.

My home.

Small circles trace against my exposed back, and I wish for this to never end. For us to be like this always. And for a few minutes, we get to feel what it always would feel like. No one bothers; time stands still while I wish for my dreams to come true. But that's the thing about dreams; they aren't real, just our minds playing tricks on us, raising hopes while life crushes them.

But I'll take these moments and remember them always.

The sound of laughing clowns and excitable children echoes in my ears. The distinct honk and then wheezing laughter give them away.

"Is my baby okay?" Beckham's words make my body tingle.

My heart nearly skips a beat as I nod into him. "Yes, I just like it here."

His arms squeeze around me tighter, keeping me safe. "Me too."

The words are simple yet powerful. He chose me, just as I chose him. Two things I'll never take for granted.

We stay together, intertwined, until a freezing gust of wind prickles our skin. Shivering, Beckham's hands rub against my skin, and I can feel the entire mood shift, not just with us but all of Fright Night.

Raising my head, I glance at the worried faces. Parents hurry their kids back toward the exit, and teenagers walk cautiously forward with uncertainty.

Looking above, my brow furrows. Clouds are moving rapidly as birds chirp, flying in flocks back to the safety of the forest.

Beckham reads my mind. "I don't know, Royce."

He says my name instead of baby. I hate when he does that, and the brat in me wants to stomp my foot, but even I can read a room. This is serious.

The wind picks up, the fabric of the tents flutters, cracking sounds fill the silence, and the rides begin to shut down. More commotion follows as the main paths fill with more people. People still fill the tents; no one peeks out, they are oblivious.

Anxiety riddles my core, the tips of my toes digging into the gravel. Something is wrong.

Just as the thought races through me, a bright white flash fills the dark black sky. Loud screams, high-pitched enough to break a mirror or glass, join as the light remains illuminating.

Beckham's hand grasps mine. "We need to go."

Shaking my head, I still don't understand.

"Baby, this one time, please, I need you to listen to me. This isn't fucking good."

The light goes out, the screams stop, and all the air from my lungs start getting sucked out. Hunching over, desperate for breath, Beckham leans with me with panic ruining his gorgeous face. Each time I try to inhale, my body deflates further, my chest begins to convulse, and tears of fear stream down my cheeks. My lungs wheeze; I am dying. With heavy eyes, I begin to collapse as my body loses all strength.

Then, suddenly, the freezing breeze comes to an end, and I'm finally able to catch a breath.

Falling to the ground, gravel sticks to my face as I lie there shamelessly. Beckham grips my face. "Holy shit, you're as pale as me... maybe even as white as a ghost, baby." He's scared. His tone tells all. And if he's scared, then I should be fucking terrified.

PRINCE

The tiny vibrations of the tattoo machine against my neck are comforting. The needle pulsates against my spine with precision and purpose. And the tongue licking my cock from base to tip is a helpful distraction from the image of *her* being fucked senseless by that vampire fucker.

Dead man walking.

I'm aware he is technically unalive, but I'll be the one to put the stake through his heart, killing him permanently.

Teeth tease my cock, soft lips following.

Predictable.

Gripping the bright pink, purple, and green hair, I push his mouth farther down. He gags, and I start fucking his face mercilessly. With hard thrusts into the back of his throat, my cock throbs.

A firm hand grips my shoulder. "Sit fucking still," the artist growls through gritted teeth.

Asshole.

Drool drips down my new friend's mouth, but I don't let up, keeping my fingers firmly intertwined in his locks.

"You don't get to breathe until I come." A little motivation for him to work harder.

My cock restricts his airway, and subtle wheezing follows from the lack of oxygen, which brings a smile to my face. On the brink of death, choking on me, what a way to die.

His head bobs desperately.

My eyes hood, captivated by the power.

As the needle on my neck releases me from its pleasure, I allow my dick to come.

Ropes coat his throat, followed by more gagging and choking. "You will fucking take it," I command, holding his head down as I ride the wave of release.

The tent surrounding us startles, rippling fabric followed by the howling of the wind. My arm hairs rise. A storm is coming.

This is all that remains of my gift, my power, the ability to detect when treacherous weather is looming ahead of time.

My balls empty, and my fingers release from the man's head, allowing him to fall backward with a flushed face.

He coughs, catching his breath with my cum mixed with saliva and tears streaming down his chin and neck.

Shoving my cock back into my trousers, I stand to zip myself up.

The tattoo artist remains sitting, rolling his eyes at me, which I pay no attention to.

"Do you want to see?" he asks. I nod once in response.

I move to the long mirror, and he follows with a smaller one facing my neck. *Her* eyes reflect back at me. Staring into my soul, burnt into my brain.

Mine.

Satisfied, I step away, taking a wad of cash out of my pocket, and I pay him. I throw a few bills at the poor fuck still on the floor before me.

"Gentlemen," is all I say before excusing myself.

Stepping outside, the carousel spins and spins, lights flashing off the figurines that children are riding on. A manic operator keeps pushing the large red button as frantic parents scream to get their children off.

The night is ominous.

My eyes shift as a flash of white light shines down upon us, feeding my soul and bringing life back into my veins. Fists clench, my chest tightens, and my muscles tense. Electricity is flowing through me as if I were hit directly by lightning.

Then it all stops. The wind. The light. The chaos.

The world is calm.

Breathing deeply through my nose, my eyes open, and a man points at me. "Oh my god, they're white."

Memories of New Orleans flash into view.

From moths fluttering around me to the humid air washing over me. Raising my arms, I embarked on a journey that changed the trajectory of my life. It's what led me to Hollows Grove, to Agatha, to what's mine. Royce. And I wouldn't change a fucking thing.

I regret nothing. I crave it all more with each day that passes. And now, the all-too-familiar feeling coursing through my veins has returned.

I am free.

9

ROYCE

"**B**aby, let me walk you home. Please," Beckham pleads.

It's not something I'm willing to further risk, since Prince has seen too much, and if Agatha knew as well, that would be the end of it all between us.

But I would take my own life before they are able to take his. I am nothing without him, and to live a life alone is no life at all.

Cuddling into his sweet embrace, I say, "I'll be okay, I promise." The words are a lie, and his body tenses, worried. He believes them as much as I do.

Witches cackle, demons ride briskly past us on unicycles, and warlocks brood with their brooms.

Looking up at the most beautiful man, I kiss his thin, cool lips for what may be the last time. He feels it too, that fact that the passion, our connection, could be compromised.

Slowly we part, his forehead resting upon mine, and hushed words are spoken so only I can hear them. "Forever mine, and I am yours. I love you, Royce."

Tears prick my eyes. Squeezing them shut, I allow one to fall. "I love you, my sweet vampire boy."

With tangled fingers, we stay like this for only a moment longer. A crack of thunder startles us.

"I should go," I painfully state.

His lips press against my forehead a final time before we separate. Sliding his fingers delicately under my dress and up my thighs, my flesh warms at his touch, along with the bite mark, which connects our souls.

Looking into his eyes, I vow, "I promise you'll see me again."

It's a lie.

I can't see Prince letting me live a life with Beckham now that he knows about him.

We disconnect.

Turning on my toes, I hoist up my dress and dash through the carnival. Weaving through bodies also fleeing, but not fast enough. I must escape before *he* finds me.

Briskly I pass through the exit gates and proceed up the hill to the forest, never looking back. Another crack of thunder follows. Looking up, the dark clouds spin as I seek shelter beneath the trees.

Panting, I stop, placing my hands on my knees and hunched over to catch my breath. I'm safe; the forest will protect me.

As my breathing becomes stable, I stand tall and follow the worn path through my home. Agatha's is where I reside, but the forest and cottage are my sanctuary of solitude. But for the first time, my home offers me a crossroads. Options and confusion. In all my years on this earth, I have only taken one way. I could close my eyes and allow instinct to guide me, and it would guide me down the same beaten road each time. But tonight a new trail has appeared; it's dark with fog dusting over the tree limbs. Each time I attempt to look away, I am pulled back, drawn to the possibilities it could present. Therefore, against all logic, giving in to curiosity and impulse, I step forward and walk down the ominous opening.

An energy pulls me forward, and I allow it to take me.

Bright eyes loom over, forest creatures watching on nervously. "I won't hurt you, precious babies." My voice is hoarse. I want to reassure them not to worry, to not fear me. I could never harm them, as I know all too well what pain feels like.

With each step, the fog parts for me, and the creatures hoot and chirp, communicating with one another, as I pass. An animal jumps over the top of my head, startling me; its paws skim the top of my head, and I freeze. It lands on the branch, and I hear it scurry up the tree trunk. I step forward and continue my journey.

Deep in, my eyes can barely see before me, and as I do, I allow instinct to take over and my feet guide me, gripping the earth with every step.

Suddenly, everything stills. All goes quiet. The forest is eerie, but I continue. The calmness my brain had with the sounds of the forest is no longer the case, and my mind begins to race. What is beyond this darkness? What lurks ahead that I cannot see? And what do they want with me?

Before my anxiety can create scenarios for each question, a loud tick fills my ears, echoing around me, and I pause. Eyes shift in an attempt to find the source, but before I do, a single sharp nail begins to slowly scrape along my exposed back.

Chills prick along my skin. A soft hiss flows from between their lips, followed by calculated clicks.

Panic sets in. My heart drops into my stomach, and my eyes begin to shift.

Refusing to turn around and face what is behind me, I shout, "Nope, not happening. Sorry!"

I'm not sure who or what I am apologizing to, but I am fucking out of here. On the tip of my toes, I scurry through the darkness; vines attempt to tickle my ankles and take a hold, but my body is in fight mode, and I don't stay still long enough to allow it. The eyes peering around me are now shifting from white and yellow to greens, reds, and blues.

More clicking fills the void, the sharp nail now moving up my scalp, where my white and black hair parts. Adrenaline keeps me moving; fear stops me from turning around.

A flash of green light floods the dark forest, and a loud shriek erupts from my mouth. I close my eyes with my hands over my ears. "Make it stop!"

The ground moves beneath me, rumbling strong enough to make my legs shake with unease.

Why is this happening?

Tears well in my eyes, and for the first time in a very long time, I am scared.

Then as quickly as it started, it stops, and I still, not moving for minutes out of fear of what I will see if I open my eyes. The phantom touch of the sharp nail can still be felt against my skin, and as I remove my hands from my ears, the ticking has ended. Slowly, lashes leave my cheeks, rising with my opening eyes.

Darkness is no more; the forest has disappeared, and as my eyes adjust, I find myself in the graveyard of Hollows Grove, standing in front of the tombstones of my mothers.

No, no, no.

Falling to my knees, the adrenaline wears off, and I allow myself to lie in the grass above their plots, plots where no bodies reside, just a symbolic location where mourning assholes can come wallow and visit the spirits of the deceased.

My fingers grip the grass. An unfamiliar faint female voice whispers, but I barely hear it, though I can feel her soft, cool lips on the shell of my ear. "Run."

With wide eyes, I rise, wasting no time, and flee.

Racing through the maze of gravestones and hedges, my legs carry me as my body is on autopilot. With no time to think, the iron gates come into view. Pumping my arms with wheezing lungs, I give it my all to get out of here before it's too late.

The sky cracks, thunder roars, and rain is next to fall.

Warm droplets hit my face. At first, it's only a drizzle, but the closer I get to the gates, the drizzle turns into a downpour, and the water droplets turn out to be red, crimson blood beading on my pale skin. The harder it falls, the beads break, streaking down my body. The taste of metal lines my tongue as I accidentally lick my lips. Red blurs my vision, but I don't let it stop me.

A large tree root trips me, and I fall on my hands, causing my face to meet the ground hard.

The blood coating my body attempts to weigh me down, making it harder to rise, and my muscles ache from exhaustion, but the adrenaline kicks in once more, aiding my escape to safety.

Never once did I think Agatha Manor would be that place, but for tonight, and only tonight, it is.

Passing through the gates, my arm brushes against the cool iron, a welcomed sensation giving me if only a second of reprieve from the blood. But the moment both my feet pass through the threshold of the graveyard, the rain stops.

Confused, I look back, only to find nothing is falling from the skies.

My chest heaves, my throat is dry, and my hands attempt to wipe my face hopelessly. Panting breathlessly, I continue racing home. Having ended up at the graveyard and not the familiar tree line I am used to it takes me longer to see the silhouette of the manor off in the distance, but it gives me hope with every step taken that I am almost safe, that the four walls will protect me.

But it still doesn't answer the question: why is this happening?

MINE!

PRINCE'S VOICE enters my head. It's loud, possessive, and terrifying.

I try to look around, find the source, but I'm greeted by wet hair slapping me in the face instead.

With my arms still pumping, they give me the momentum I need to reach the manor.

Just as I make it to the back door, his voice invades my mind once more.

WE WILL MAKE the world dance for us.

·   ·   ·

SCREAMING INTO THE NIGHT, exhausted and on the brink of a nervous fucking breakdown, I shriek, "Get out of my head!"

The door is unlocked, and it opens as I turn the brass knob. Stepping inside, darkness greets me, comfort fills my body, and I hope this house does the one thing it has never done before... protect me.

10

ROYCE

Submerging my body under the lukewarm water, I lie in the tub with my eyes wide open, looking up at the ceiling. Agatha's bedroom door was closed as I peered down the hall, and the rest of the house was quiet, with no sign of Prince.

Hiding in my blood-red bathroom, I started a bath, where I am now decompressing inside.

When I first saw my reflection as the water filled the tub, I was mortified. It was horrific. If anyone were to have seen me, they would have thought I was fleeing the scene of a mass murder. Not an inch of my body was free of blood, the top of my dress barely keeping my breasts covered due to the weight of it. My purple eyes were the only contrast other than my teeth when I opened my mouth in shock.

Sliding the thin straps off my shoulders, I let my dress fall off my body, bunched around my feet, on the floor, where it remains now.

My lungs contract the longer I stay underwater without oxygen, and my arms shake as I stop them from reaching up to grip the sides of the porcelain tub. Counting back from five, I decide if I make it to one, I will get up, but I take my time in doing so.

Five.

I try to calm my mind.

Four.

If I were to attempt to process the events of tonight, it would only cause me to spiral further.

Three.

What is meant to be will conquer.

GET UP!

His voice is back, and my body shoots up out of the water. My lungs gasp, taking in the air they so desperately were begging for with my eyes wide open. The cool edge of the bathtub grounds me as I sit here in shock.

A loud whimper catches my attention. Slowly, my eyes trace over the red subway tiles against the wall. The black countertop is bare, but the edge displays familiar hands.

In a cream milkmaid-style dress, the corset

cinched around the waist and the hem ruffled at the hips, *his* cock forcefully fills her from behind as he holds her head... *my* head forward, forcing me to watch through the reflection of the mirror.

With kicking legs, I attempt to force him off of me.

Bucking back has zero effect. He likes it, grinning widely and daring me to continue.

"I hate you!" I snarl.

His voice is low, and his response is short but powerful. "Good."

Fresh cuts decorate my bare arms, red stains my white hair. I am horribly broken and an easy prey for my tormentor.

Loud grunts overshadow the whimpers of distress, and the black bathroom door steadily opens. An old lady with boring brown garments stands in the opening, watching, emotionless. My purple eyes move their focus in the mirror to her, to Agatha, pleading for her to help me, but she does nothing. She stands, still watching, still emotionless. Agatha was never an ally, yet for a moment I had hope.

Hope for her to save me, this one fucking time.

With a curt nod, her black leather trainers step

back, and she walks away, leaving me exposed to the demon.

He is her pet, but if he only knew how tight of a leash he was on.

I hate them both.

His warm cum coats my bare ass. Watching, I can see my lip trembling in the mirror. His teeth become exposed even more, satisfied by my response.

Shrieking, I can't hold it in any further. "You're a monster!"

Prince's teeth graze my shoulder. "And your worst fucking nightmare, sweet Royce."

This part is embedded in my memory, as humiliation riddles through me, and the memory plays out before me. Warm urine trickles on my feet. He's released his bladder onto me. "You are nothing to no one. I own you. You are my fucking property, and I will do anything I fucking like with you."

My foster brother's words sting; tears prick my eyes, but that's when a wave of clarity washes over me. This is what he wants, my pain, my fear, my embarrassment.

He will never fucking get it again.

As Prince tucks himself into his trousers, because this tool has always worn a suit, his dress shoes click against the tile floor, and he leaves me defiled and degraded.

I watch as my fist slams against the mirrored glass. It shatters, cutting into the side of my hand. Unfazed, blood-coated fingers reach for a large, sharp piece which has fallen upon the countertop. Twisting my arm, I expose my upper inner arm; the sensitive, thin skin is pale and untouched. And without a second thought, I shove the tip of the sharp glass into my flesh. This is the first time I am cutting downward instead of diagonally. With purpose, but still cowering in fear, as no major artery will be touched. With no hesitation, I continue moving until I hit the crook of my elbow, blood dripping rapidly down, mixing with the urine at my feet. I am a fucking mess, but I couldn't care less.

Once satisfied, I drop the bloodied, shattered mirror shard into the sink beside me and stare back at the reflection of myself.

I win.

He loses.

Because my inner strength is stronger than his fucking pompous asshole facade with those moronic teardrop tattoos by his eye.

Prince gets off on making me feel small, meanwhile I get off on never giving him what he wants.

Oh, foster brother, we can both play games, but little do you know I am better at them than you, and I will fucking win because I am in this for the long haul. Motherfucker.

Then before my eyes, my body turns to smoke, fading away.

The bath is ice cold now, and I am staring off into a blank space.

Tilting my head, my eyes take in the white, raised scar from that day years ago. Each scar represents a moment in my life of great significance. Positive or negative, I don't discriminate. This one was a mixture of both.

Pulling my focus, my hand reaches forward, gripping the claw knob for the bath. Twisting, it squeaks, before releasing the warm water into the cool tub. I feel it first on my feet and legs; lying back, I revel in the relief it brings me. The pipes vibrate against the wall, muffled grumbles join, and I roll my eyes. I can't wait for Jerry to fix them.

The balls of my feet rub against my legs, helping the warm water mix into the cold. I do this back and forth a few times before my face turns. The smell of metal begins to overwhelm my nostrils. Once thin, moving water between my toes feels thick and slimy.

Slanting my head to the side, I open my shut

eyes, and the room is as it was when I first arrived. No one lurks in the doorway, no one waiting to torture me. Hesitantly, I shift back to the tub, glancing down at my exposed breasts with perky nipples; they are submerged in the water no more.

Blood.

So much fucking blood.

In a panic, my foot kicks up; my toes try to unplug the drain as I reach forward to turn the water off. Removing my toes, the flow of crimson subsides, yet I still hear the sound of dripping. I look around, confused.

An audible gasp leaves me. The once-scarred cuts decorating my arms have split open. A loud scream of terror follows. *Why is this happening*?

Jumping out of the porcelain tub, my feet slip and slide against the matching crimson tile floor. Reaching for my towel, I nearly go ass over head, latching onto the towel rack. It helps prevent my fall.

Once I'm somewhat calmed, I stand tall and begin to try and stop the bleeding by applying pressure on the wounds with the towel. Looking into the mirror, dark circles surround my purple eyes. My bones protrude; I look so incredibly frail. Vulnerable. Scared. Just how *he* likes me.

Then, a quick flash startles me further, and he appears, standing behind my reflection, smiling.

"Boo!"

I jump, startled.

Then *he* is gone.

Looking down, my arms are no longer bloodied; the cuts are closed. My body is as it was.

But the obvious remains.

Something terrible is coming.

11

PRINCE

A delicate flower.

My choice of poison.

My foster sister.

Royce.

And now she gets to see me for all that I am.

For all that I am capable of.

The sound of hurried feet echo above me, followed by the swift closing of the door. Rolling my eyes, her efforts to evade me are useless.

I will always find her.

Creep into her thoughts, dreams, and subconscious effortlessly.

To make her remember everything her brain has attempted to block and protect her from. For Royce, my sweet Royce, to be reminded that I fucking own her.

Since the starting days of our time together, my body needed to possess hers.

Her sadness brought me joy. And when I tormented her, it got me hard.

Still does.

So even as a child, I would destroy all the things she loved, including the tree swing where she first sat and watched me walk up the path and into this forsaken place.

Royce cried for days after I cut the branch down. Agatha locked her inside of her room for days, but only because the crying annoyed her and Royce wouldn't stop.

She was given no food or water the entire time. And aiding her never crossed my mind.

My punishment was being kept from her and being unable to see her absolutely destroyed in person, only to hear it through her door and the thin walls.

Grumbles of distress bring me back to the present. Glancing at the corner of the living room, black leather shoes dangle, their feet off the ground. My own are resting nicely on top of a coffee table as I lean back in a plush reading chair.

Raking my fingers through my disheveled white hair, my mind searches the house for Royce, who seems to be prolonging our night of broken bodies. Still in her room, sitting before her vanity with her head resting in her hands. Shoulders shaking. She's crying.

We don't have time for this.

I haul the stool back, causing her bare legs to fly out, her head rising and her fingers gripping the seat.

YOU ARE WASTING MY TIME.

FRANTICALLY, she looks around the space, attempting to find the source of my voice.

YOU WILL NOT FIND me in your room because I occupy your mind, my sweet Royce.

Now come to me.

STANDING TALL, her body is naked, pussy bare.

Stepping forward, I watch as she steps delicately forward. Her body is exquisite.

I will devour her, mark her, and control her.

Swinging the door open for her, the force blows her hair back. Royce's face is neutral, no expression, and although the tears have stopped, I feel her anxiety vibrating through each bone and breath.

Bringing her down the hall and to the stairs, her footsteps are loud.

Her dramatics fall on deaf ears as I don't react, yet.

As she reaches the bottom, she takes in our guest of honor hanging freely in the corner of the living room. Anxiety is now turning into full-on panic. I cannot relinquish my control over her yet; she'll try to run, and I am in no mood to chase.

Waving my arms out wide, I cheerfully welcome Royce. "So glad you can finally join us. Agatha, why don't you tell us a fun ghost story?" Loud, wicked laughter follows. I am whole, and those who tried to suppress me shall pay.

"You ungrateful bastard," she hisses back.

I tsk her. "Tell us a thrilling tale. Perhaps a tale of why our abilities vanished the moment you entered our lives and took us in?"

I allow Agatha to ponder this as a knife floats in the air, teasing her neck.

Forcefully, I pull Royce to stand before me.

Her petite, naked body is on display for me. My eyes take her in from head to toe, and my cock twitches against my trousers. Leaning forward, my hand cups her pussy, and it's dry.

"You fucking bitch," I snide.

SIT!

HER BODY JOLTS FORWARD, then folds onto my lap stiffly.

My hand returns to her pussy, the tips of my fingers circle her clit, and just as I am about to bring my mouth to her hard pink nipples, *it* catches my attention.

A mark I have never seen before on her inner thigh.

She has plenty of scars. But this one is unique and not one of her own making.

Teeth.

Rage fills my veins. My fingernails embed themselves into her sensitive nub.

His fucking teeth.

Agatha chokes, gagging from the force I'm applying around her neck. The sharp tip of the knife twitches as I debate using it next.

"He's dead," I state plainly, my face stoic.

My hold over Royce vanishes, and she rapidly rises from my lap and attempts to scurry away from me.

I fucking think not.

The pads of her feet are harsh against the floor; her leg rises to take the first step up the staircase, but I stop her, throwing her helpless body back and slamming it against the front door. Her head thuds loudly as the rest of her body follows, connecting against the hardwood, as the wind is knocked out of her. Her lungs wheeze as she collapses to the floor, her body lying limp on the dark decorative rug.

Beneath her brave exterior, Royce is nothing more than a fucking piece of meat, which I will ravish night after fucking night. There is no need to break her, because she is already so very broken. And I will remind her each day and every night just how worthless she is.

I rise while Agatha still gasps for air, so I allow some to enter her lungs as I stand above Royce. My words come out like venom as I taunt her unconscious body, "Because you will never forget you were the one who killed your moms. Your moms who can't even bring themselves to see you in the afterlife." I spit on her as the last word leaves my lips.

Stepping back, I spot the small door under the stairs that leads to the small cold room and get an idea. Throwing my head back, I chuckle hysterically.

I am fucking back. I am free.

"Oh, my pet, we are about to have so much fun together."

12

ROYCE

My body trembles, and my head aches from behind my eyes down to my spine.

Chills envelop me. Unable to bring myself to move, I keep seeing *him*.

His eyes shone a bright white as his mind controlled mine. Evil radiated from his aura.

Then my stomach drops.

Fuck.

Prince saw my mate's mark. Beckham is now in danger because of me. Dread looms over me like a dark cloud, like the blood rain that terrorized me earlier this evening.

To be responsible for yet another death of someone who is my family, I won't survive it.

. . .

BUT I WILL MAKE YOU.

I STARTLE.

His voice is haunting. And it's now evident that my thoughts are no longer safe, and perhaps not even my own.

AND I AM GOING to make you watch.

OPENING MY EYES, I brace for the intrusion of brightness but awaken to darkness instead. For that, I am thankful. The ground beneath me is hard, cold cement. In an attempt to get my bearings, my torso rises slightly, but not even a crack of light is peeking through.

Touching my body, I feel a harsh, scratchy fabric against me. A men's undershirt. It's uncomfortable, but I am no longer exposed, which is a relief.

As I attempt to stand, I am quickly stopped by the low ceiling above me. My head hits it instantly, triggering the sharp pain in my head to intensify. I wince, lowering myself back down on the hard floor, squeezing my eyes shut, wishing it would stop.

The feeling of exhaustion washes over me, and I let out a large yawn, allowing sleep to take over. The multiple head traumas have most likely left me concussed, and I shouldn't give in to the slumber, but to fight it only feels as if it will take more energy from me.

Heads or Tails?

THE VOICE, which now haunts my dreams, wakes me. The concept of time has evaded me; darkness and nightfall are all that live here.

A hushed whisper leaves my dry mouth, "I won't play your games."

Defiance gets his dick hard, and ultimately I lose either way, so if to defy him means I am being true to myself, I will fight his wickedness.

"Please, baby, pick."

The words sound pained, and my eyes shoot open.

"Don't you fucking touch him!" I scream, and it sends sharp knife-like pain into my skull, but I will sacrifice myself for him in any way I can.

. . .

WHAT HAPPENS NEXT IS up to you. Heads or Tails?

AND THAT INCLUDES GIVING in to his fucking games.
My voice shakes nervously. "Tails."

I ALWAYS LIKED the long game. To watch as they do what I command.

MY BROW FURROWS IN CONFUSION. Rage courses through me. And I am suddenly very awake. The sharp pain stabbing in my skull dissipates as my focus centers on Beckham.
"Prince! You motherfucker!"
An evil cackle follows.

I WISH, but sadly both of yours are dead.

TIME PASSES SLOWLY, or does it?

Hours or days or weeks—I don't have a clue how long it's been.

The concept of time doesn't exist here, wherever *here* is.

Sitting up on my knees, I place both hands above my head until they connect with the ceiling. What's above is as hard and cold as what I sit on. I move my fingers around the space. Surely there has to be an opening, an entrance somewhere. I didn't magically just end up in a hole, or did I?

Claustrophobia hits me like a tidal wave. Panic sends my mind into a tailspin. I feel as if I have just fallen through ice, in the middle of a lake, on a cold winter's day. Freezing water sucks me in and feels like a thousand knives piercing my skin.

Hypothermia.

Opening my eyes, I look up, hands against the ice, unable to find the hole that I just plummeted through. Rapidly, I search and search, letting my last air bubble out, and my body weeps as I begin to fade. All hope is gone, and I let myself go, drifting off to the depths of no return.

And that is exactly how this feels, slapping the palms of my hands against the cold cement ceiling, hopelessly. Until I give one last bang, pleading, "Please," and squeaky hinges respond.

Relief allows my body to relax. Sliding my hands above, a sharp edge catches my skin, telling me it's wood. It's a small wood door.

Then realization washes over me. Shit, I'm in a cold storage space. It's the only thing that makes sense, with how tiny it is and the location of the overhead door. But how the fuck do I get out of it? I didn't even know the manor had one of these.

And as I think about the manor, Agatha's floating body comes to the forefront of my mind. A silver knife angled so perfectly at her thick throat. One movement and it would slice her open and release all life from her.

I would not mourn her, nor would I cry. A celebration of death would be held as I burned this forsaken place to the ground. No other child should have to be placed here or put through her wrath. And as much as I hate Prince, he didn't deserve her shit either, because he was just a child; he could have been saved.

Prince was her favorite out of the two of us. You wouldn't be able to tell immediately because she strived to make us both miserable and obedient, but my punishments were always worse than his. And Prince has always been suspicious of her but never acted on it until now.

He loves a long game, to watch and wait. To play them like a fucking fiddle and then laugh as they burn is his specialty. Just as he did with his parents before their untimely ending.

And with this one simple thought, his voice invades my inner sanctum once more.

CLOSE YOUR EYES *and come on this ride with me.*

I TRY TO RESIST, but his abilities force them shut.

Heavy breathing fills my ears.

With my bare feet against the cool floor, I push my seated body backward.

Who is in here with me?

The hard wall hits sooner than expected, startling me. I gasp, freezing from fear.

A loud chuckle vibrates in the small space, only frightening me further.

Gripping my hair, I pull it hard at the roots, bringing my focus to the pain instead of terror. I find comfort in pain. Peace returns to me and the heavy breathing subsides, and that's when it occurs to me... I was the one panting, breathing so heavily that I scared myself.

Being kept in the dark, alone, is starting to fuck with me.

I pull my hair harder, keeping my mind in the present, focused on the now, not allowing it to run away too far out of my reach. Just as I calm myself somewhat, the distinct ringing of our doorbell excites me.

Help is coming.

Loud bangs in quick succession follow as I see Prince arrogantly walking toward the door. He doesn't bother looking through the peephole before opening it, rubbing the palms of his hands together. I get the feeling he knows who it is. I'm curious. I didn't think Prince knew people.

With the creak of the old, un-oiled hinges, the door opens wide.

And in plain view is someone who shouldn't fucking be at our front door.

Releasing my hair, with a closed fist, I slam the sides of my hands into the cement walls.

"You shouldn't be here! Why are you here?" I scream in a fit of rage with saliva spitting out of my mouth. Some drips down my chin, and I allow it, because it doesn't matter.

None of it matters if *he* is here.

Abruptly, the throbbing pain of my headache

returns behind my eyes, but it doesn't stop my emotions from flowing because another scream follows, and now it feels like there is a sharp knife stabbing me directly in the pupil of my eye.

Their mouths move, but my ears have stopped working. White noise fills my head, mixed in with the distant slapping sound of flesh pounding the wall.

Breaking slowly. My soul has a crack in its foundation, and my heart weeps.

Snot and tears mix with my drool. Why is he here?

Prince pulls him in without even touching him. His feet scrape against the floor, and the door slams, shaking the walls and frames decorating them.

Defeat absorbs into my body; a wallow of sorrow follows. "Baby, why did you come?"

Prince doesn't just pull Beckham in; he slams his body into the staircase banister, the edge directly thrusting itself into his gut and causing him to immediately bring up bile.

Thick black locks fall over Beckham's forehead as he is thrown backward into the wall behind him, knocking the wind out of him. His head bounces, and I wince, but it doesn't stop there. The knife previously used on Agatha flies forward and comes within millimeters of Beck's chest, just over his heart.

No!

My body slides down the wall until I am lying on my back.

My feet take me forward until I reach the other side of the small prison cell I've been placed in. The ticking of the clock from the living room takes over the space where white noise once lived. It's toying with me. Motherfucker.

Raising my legs, I use my feet to feel for the door.

Prince taunts Beckham as he hangs in the air, and he slowly inches toward him, teasing, "I can taste your death, and I promise you, it is beautiful."

Beckham's bright white, sharp canines are on display, his muscles contracting in his neck and eyes going from dark brown to a vibrant red. And my foster brother has the audacity to place his hand around his neck, squeezing tight. "First, I'll starve you. Make you crave crimson. Then enter a state of delusion and frenzy. *Her* scent will send you into a tailspin. And as much as it would pain me to witness such an event, you would be unable to stop as you drink her dry. Killing your mate and being left to live with it for an eternity." Prince pauses, chuckling at his perverse fantasy. "That would *almost* be better than killing you myself."

Sick bastard. He would relish something so inhumane and vile. With his cock in hand and a giant smile on his face, this is the kind of shit that gets him off.

My face turns, disgusted.

Then, just as Prince releases Beckham's throat, I notice something peeking out of the collar of his suit, just under his hairline at the back of his neck. It is an obvious addition next to his white blond hair because dark long lashes are connected to electrifying purple eyes... my fucking eyes. Without a doubt in my mind, I know they are mine.

Sparkle has been added, giving them more life than the set I live with each day.

He is sick. Fucking unwell.

Reaching into his pant pocket, Prince pulls out a string of black beads. Confused, I wait. This man does nothing at random; everything is always carefully plotted with purpose. Instead of turning away and returning his focus to Agatha, who is still floating in the living room, his hand moves rapidly. Sizzle and smoke follow.

Beckham screams in agony. His eyes squeeze

shut while his body twitches, trying to break free from the hold Prince has over him.

As Prince's hand falls back, the clear imprint of a crucifix is etched into Beckham's face.

The skin is blistering and bright red, and it doesn't fucking end.

Prince has a rosary in his hands, and he will use it until it's no longer fun.

Slamming my feet into the wooden door of the cold storage, I can't sit and watch this any further. He is torturing us both and reveling in it.

I am not a strong person, physically and mentally, most of the time, so with one hard kick, the door doesn't fly off. Repeatedly, I use all my might. The lock jingles while the hinges creak.

"Baby, I'm coming. I promise," I murmur to myself with each strike.

Breathlessly, my chest heaves, and my mouth becomes parched. My brain is losing the will to continue this tedious task, but my body and heart will not give up on him.

With each kick of my boot, I hear parts of the hinge rattling. And I hope it's been poorly screwed in and is on the verge of popping off.

A thunderous roar erupts from me. Giving it my fucking all, I muster every ounce of energy I can find in my final attempt at escape. My feet surge forward as the screws of the thin metal hinge fly off and the door swings open.

Coughing, my throat is dry, but I attempt to catch my breath.

Meanwhile, Prince's head turns. He's heard me.

Excitement turns to dread.

In one brisk movement, I roll over onto my stomach, my nose brushing against the dusty, cool floor. I hold my breath to stop a sneeze, then push myself up into a squat before gripping the edge above me and hoisting my frail, aching body up.

With my eyes still forced closed, I use my hands to feel around the room I am currently standing in, and my worst worry is falling ass over feet back into that fucking hole. Therefore, standing is not an option. Sliding my feet in short spurts is the only way. My heart beats rapidly under my chest as time is racing against me.

Then, Beckham's burning face returns before me. You can no longer tell it's a crucifix destroying him; it's all blending into one large wound.

"Take me. Hurt me. Hate me!" I scream. "Let me take his pain, please!"

Prince's head whips around, his deranged eyes looking back at me. "Never."

If he can hear me, he knows I'm coming and won't be able to stop me.

Nothing with him is easy.

Dread falls over me because I know it's only going to get worse.

My hands find the single doorknob, and I attempt to turn it, but it doesn't budge. He has me locked in.

Adrenaline begins to take over. I am so close.

Putting all my momentum behind it, I slam my body into the door separating us.

Prince drops the rosary at the exact same time, and it slowly falls to his feet.

I slam my body once more.

With shrugging shoulders, he casually says, "Fuck it."

Confused, I pause and watch.

Prince hops down the steps and saunters over to the record player.

What is he doing?

Kicking the leg out of the wooden record player stand, it flies off, and the records crash to the floor.

Kneeling, Prince takes the broken leg into his hand and spins around on the balls of his black dress shoes.

A renewed sense of urgency washes over me. *Don't you fucking dare!*

This time Prince doesn't respond to me.

Reaching the banister, he twirls with joy, a state I have never seen him in before, and I want to be sick. My stomach turns as I bash the door down and fall on top of it, hitting the ground.

Scrambling, I get to my feet, and I think my vision has returned, because before me is the fallen record player stand.

Wasting no time, I run to Beckham. But it's too late. I am too fucking late.

The knife, which was once floating millimeters from penetrating his heart, is gone and it has been replaced with Prince's hand and the wooden stake.

Prince looks over to me and winks as Beckham's hand takes his spot.

Frantic, I think, what is he doing?

I try to get to him, but I find myself only able to run in one place.

Why is this happening?

Prince holds both hands up in the air as Beckham's arm reaches out, still holding the sharp piece of wood at chest level.

It happens in slow motion.

Denial and disbelief wash over me.

My mate slams the stake into his own heart, and by default, my own.

Breaking it into a million unfixable pieces.

Crippled, my lifeless body collapses to my knees.

A familiar feminine voice is screeching around us. It seems so far away, like a haunting soundtrack playing while my heart breaks.

Perhaps it's me, but I can't tell because I am numb.

Beckham's body crumbles down the stairs, his eyes still open, but the vivid red is now dull. His skin has gone from a beautiful, pale white with exposed, shimmery tattoos to a deathly gray.

"But I'm not done yet, sweet girl." I hate him.

My mind tells me the only way to feel better, or to not feel at all, is to join him.

Because the only person to make me feel whole since my moms passed, was him, Beckham. My vampire boy.

Fading away, I lie here lifelessly. Until I am forced to move.

Prince.

The front door is still open, and I am tossed through it and lifted two stories to the roof. And instead of dropping me, Prince forces my legs to straighten, but I fight him until the very end. I will not make anything easy for him. With tense muscles, my teeth grit.

Dark clouds still circle overhead, and moths flutter around my lifeless body, tickling my bare skin with their wings and antennas.

Then, all at once, they leave me, revealing my worst nightmare come to life.

"So beautiful, just like my mama in the garden."

Looking over to the devil beside me, his eyes, still bright white, are in a trancelike state.

Swallowing hard, his Adam's apple bobs, and his face radiates happiness.

He must feel me focusing on him because I am just as quickly forced back to seeing the heartache in the garden. Beckham.

Maggots and centipedes wiggle and crawl over his body. Dead, brown, brittle shrubs surround him, attempting to steal his light and his beauty. But they can't have it. No one can. I want to fight the brown vines intertwining around his limbs, but I know it's of no use. Prince would stop me from jumping.

The stake is missing. Instead, cockroaches climb out of the vacant hole.

Please, make it stop, I plead internally.

And I think Prince can hear me because slowly, he turns his head. And with mischief in his voice, he asks, "Are you ready for the ghost story?"

13

PRINCE

Having had my fun playing with Royce's fragile mind, it's now time to focus on the queen cunt, Agatha. That dirty, dumb bitch is going to talk today and tell us a story for the ages. A story which will haunt my pet ever so perfectly. Resentment will build further, breaking her while under my thumb.

Speaking of my pet, I glance over to her and roll my eyes.

Royce is currently collapsed, wallowing in a wave of grief, now that we are back inside.

Snot hangs off her nose, saliva webs across her open lips, and tears sneak out from behind her closed eyes.

Smirking, I enjoy watching Royce in her most fragile state of mind. Licking my sharp teeth, I watch in amusement, wondering when she will realize the hold I had over her has been released. And as disappointed as I am that she was able to get out of the cold cellar under the stairs, it all ended up working out.

Walking over to Royce, I kick her pathetic, frail body, and she whimpers in distress.

Her body is just as weak as her mind.

Easily manipulated, moldable by my hands, and a believer when I tell her just how worthless she is. All her self-loathing she thinks I know nothing about, but behind closed doors it is all I envision when stroking my giant cock. To her name.

Leaning over, my fingers intertwine with the base of her scalp, gripping her two-toned locks tightly.

"Get the fuck up," I spit while dragging her up, yanking her hair forcefully enough that I can feel the roots pulling out of her scalp where they are deeply embedded.

Royce's dainty hands reach up and wrap around my fist. "No, no. It hurts. Stop."

Her pleas fall on deaf ears.

Dark makeup streams down her rosy cheeks.

And as I yank her across the floor, the shirt I put her in rolls up, exposing her bare bottom and pussy. Her feet kick in another attempt to resist my power, but my control is the only thing keeping her grounded.

Swollen eyes look up at me, but pity will not be given, nor will remorse be felt.

Reaching Agatha, I toss Royce beneath her floating feet, watching as her head bounces off the wall. Followed by a loud wallow. With no patience for her, I step forward and place my black leather dress shoe on top of her face, applying pressure while looking disapprovingly down at her. "No tears, or screams, will make this stop." I pause, smirking down at her while applying more pressure, squeezing her face tighter between my foot and the floor. Her head has to be killing her, I think, while cackling into the room. "In fact, it's only going to make all this more interesting."

Stepping on her head harder, I apply more pressure with glee before pushing off of her. The imprint of my custom leather shoes shines in the bright red against her pale skin. I step back, and I admire the spectacle before me. Holding my arms out, my head falls back as I bask in the glory which I have single-handedly created.

Perhaps pride is flooding my ego. It's not an arrogant ego; it's an earned and deserved one. Because just fucking look at what I am capable of.

It's masterful.

My name may be Prince, but I am a fucking king.

"Agatha, slippery and slimy. Your oath to protect those who you take into your care has been broken time and time again," I taunt, tsking her. And having the knife tease her eyeball, it circles slowly in small, intentional movements.

My body relaxes. The fun is only just beginning.

I unbutton my white dress shirt further before sitting back down in my chair with my legs propped up, crossed at the ankles. My index finger points at her, and my voice commands, "Talk!"

Agatha holds back, her face expressing that she has no fucks to give.

"You will stay up there, hanging, as you starve to death, and as your mouth becomes parched, my piss will be the only thing to quench it." Pounding my fist down on the armrest, I demand respect and force her mouth to move whilst I shout out of frustration, "SPEAK, YOU FUCKING BITCH, SPEAK! YOU KNOW WHAT YOU DID TO ME THAT NIGHT!" My breath is heavy as I struggle to contain my composure.

.   .   .

ADMIT IT.

WITH DAZED EYES, Agatha's wrinkled, skinny lips move, and her vocal cords produce her nails-to-a-chalkboard voice.

"A suppression spell. It was a suppression spell, dammit." The words are spat out like venom, and my gaze stills on Royce to observe her reaction.

And from here on out, Agatha can only speak the truth, so help her Satan.

My sweet foster sister had better be listening.

No movements or hitches in breath; instead, she lies still, while Agatha continues. "The same spell I cast on all your foster siblings. None of you are worthy of your gifts."

And who made you judge and jury? I want to inquire while knowing all too well how hypocritical the question is, considering my history; therefore, I resist the temptation.

"That ungrateful cunt, laying pathetically on the floor, battered and wallowing in self-pity, snuck into your room that night. I wasn't done. She interrupted us just as she did when she killed her mothers. She can never keep her nose out of other people's business."

Raising a brow, I am intrigued, so I encourage her to continue.

GO ON.

"I HAD one spell left to cast as your body levitated and your light seeped out. With the door opening, it broke my concentration. My eyes made contact with hers, causing your body to drop to your bed, and like a coward, *she* fled, leaving nothing but despair and disappointment in her path."

Squinting my eyes, I search my memory, attempting to force myself to remember, as Agatha narrates our stroll down memory lane.

"*Au casha, brute casha. Don heir see kata, brame heir se more,*" Agatha's words hushed out,

hissed and spoken with intention.

ENOUGH GAMES. *Explain!*

. . .

"THE LAST STEP in suppressing your thoughts. To remove your ability to remanence. You would flourish at the memory of your horrific and heinous acts. I was protecting the world from your kind and hers. You are not worthy to live among us. I would have killed you both if the counsel allowed one to get away with it."

Royce's hands tremble against the hard floor. And her voice is a barely audible whisper. "You don't get to decide that."

"I fucking do, and you should be grateful I even took you in. I could have left you for death. Rotting in that filth you visit when you don't think I'm watching. Everything *he* has done to you has been deserved."

Rubbing my palms together, the plot thickens, and excitement slithers through me as I am simply delighted.

"You killed two of the highest-ranking witches in their coven, at the university, and maybe the world. You deserve nothing but pain. A long, drawn-out suffering from my hand to your mind. Happiness was never going to be on the menu for you." Agatha is on a roll, but perhaps she's forgotten who I am and what Royce is to me.

I bring her tears. Ignite fear and carve self-hate into her arms.

Interjecting before Agatha attempts to steal *my* show, I spit, "But the spell was broken, and I reminisced often and held great resentment toward you, old lady. Because I always knew you had something to do with it. With our abilities ceasing to exist as they once did." Rising to my feet, I clasp my hands together and rejoice. "And thanks to the powers that be, I am fucking free."

Agatha scoffs, disgusted. "The white witch who mourns in the graveyard. Her fit has caused havoc upon us."

The white witch, who is draped from head to toe in white garments and pure white hair, is someone you can go to for aid, along with another witch, who dresses in all black, but they are too unpredictable to be trusted, in my opinion, and often have a high price requested in return for such assistance.

Because several times over the long, aching years under the roof of Agatha's manor, I would toy with the idea of going to them to help me get back what I rightfully was born with, something that was unrightfully taken. But I resisted because I knew the price would be unimaginable. Once they knew what

I desired, they would hold it against me and over me until I paid up.

The taunting and teasing would cause the temptation to run rampant, but I remain thankful that I always resisted. And now all those who tormented me while passing the manor as I played outside as a boy will get what they fucking deserve. Our time has come, and it's too late to run.

A dry cough from Royce brings back my attention to the present, her words softly spoken with purpose. "It's why your eyes shine bright."

Nodding, I agree.

The curse has been removed, and now I thrive.

Swiftly, I saunter back to the broken girl lying hopelessly on the ground. Kneeling back down, my fingers adjust Royce's hair, sweeping it off her face, as I whisper wickedly into her ear, "And when this bitch dies, so does your suppression spell."

Her eyes open wide, and she is suddenly very alert.

The words I've just spoken could be a lie. I have no proof of them being facts. But hope has returned, and if it fails once Agatha falls, Royce's sorrow will belong to me.

. . .

WATCH THIS.

I RISE. Stepping back, I slip both hands into my trouser pockets.

Smiling sinfully, I begin.

"Royce! Stand the fuck up." I kick her side, encouraging her to obey. The tip of my shoe connects with her ribs. The force from the impact forces her body to slide back, and I hear her ribs crack, much to my delight.

She winces, and my cock hardens once more. Tapping my head, I encourage him to calm down. Soon, he will get to play too.

To my dismay, Royce doesn't rise.

Sweeping my own hair back off my forehead, I force her to join me in witnessing the great fall of Agatha within her manor.

Staring deeply, I pull Royce up, placing her on her bare feet next to me. As my hold releases, she crumbles. Bending over, I grip her arm, and through gritted teeth, I threaten, because if she continues to test me, I will do it, "You will be fucking present for this. Your disobedience will not be tolerated. I will make you rewatch, on repeat, what I did to your vampire."

Sniffles of sadness follow, and my eyes roll while yanking her back up.

Hunched over, she babies her left side with trembling hands. "I'm here. I'm fucking here. Watching. Is this what you wanted from me? Are you happy now?"

Immensely, I silently say to myself.

TAKE THE KNIFE. *From ear to ear. And be sure to not shed a tear.*

AGATHA'S wilted old hand wraps around the black handle of the chef's knife. Casually, she brings it down from her eye and places the sharp tip on the side of her face, beside her tragus. Forcefully, she impales herself. The knife makes a clean cut as she drags it across her face. Blood begins to bead out, staining her face, running down onto her vile brown frock. Some crimson leaves droplets on the floor beneath her.

Smiling, my white teeth show, unable to suppress the glee coming over me as I watch her demise by my hand... my fucking mind.

Glancing at Royce, her stare is toward Agatha's feet. That will not fucking do.

My hand grips her face, squeezing her cheeks. I can feel her molars against my fingers. The overwhelming desire to lick her face washes over me, and I do, deliberately, all the way up to the corner of her eye. My teeth nip, and my lips move against her skin. "You will watch."

Royce attempts to swallow, then trembles before nodding yes.

Releasing my hold, I reward her with a muttered "Good girl," then return my focus back to Agatha, who has made the cut all the way to the corner of her lip.

Taking the knife, she swipes it between her teeth and continues to slice the other side. Through her cheek and muscle, her jawbone and molars can be seen. Blood is profusely gushing out of her now, but not enough to kill her, just for her to choke on.

Her face is carved, and her chin is stained. The droplets of crimson are turning into an exquisite puddle that I wish to bathe in later.

DROP THE KNIFE.

. . .

AGATHA'S HAND releases the blade. It falls to the side, bouncing off the floor several times before finally settling with a clatter.

My hand wraps around Royce's tiny wrist, and her feet trip over one another as I drag her behind me to the kitchen. With great force and pleasure, I rapidly move Agatha ahead of us, then slam her body against the cold tiled floor while reciting this poem.

DANCING AND PRANCING to the wood stove oven we go,
    One hop, two hops, three hops, we watch it glow.
    And as you burn, the sweet scent of death,
    Karma came to you. Now rot with the rest.

AGATHA RISES. Blood continues flowing from her as she reaches up to the shelf above the forest green cast iron stove. A box of matches is gripped tightly in her hand. Sliding it open, she takes a match and swiftly swipes it in order to ignite it.

Bending over, she opens the small door next to the oven where the wood rests, then tosses the lit match onto the chopped logs.

Oxygen feeds the fire, and we keep the door open until the flames roar to life.

Once satisfied, I tell her to close the door, and we resume watching the orange and red vibrantly flicker through the glass window.

HOP IN, hop now.
Burn, bitch, burn.

THE MAIN OVEN DOOR OPENS; it too has a glass window for us to view inside. Agatha steps in as the space heats up. The fit will be tight, but I will force her in if that's what it takes.

A second foot follows, and she begins to shimmy her body backward, placing her hands on the ground as support. My heart races with excitement as I pull Royce closer to me. "It's beautiful, isn't it?" The question is rhetorical, and my eyes are captivated with delight.

Agatha hunches over, squeezing her head through the opening and wrapping her arms around her bent knees that are digging into her chest. She just barely fits.

. . .

CLOSE!

THE DOOR SLAMS SHUT, then the latch follows, securing it to remain shut. The iron cylinder attached to it helps move the smoke outside as the fire gets bigger and the oven becomes hotter. Some hot air remains trapped, fogging the glass periodically as we watch her suffocate. Sweat drips, mixed with the blood. The sweet sizzling of her hands against the oven walls is soothing.

I don't allow her to scream or beg for release.

She will sit there and fucking take it, just as I did when she suppressed my abilities.

Tilting my head, I peek over to Royce to ensure she is watching, and for the first time all evening I find her enjoying her time with me. With wide eyes, the flickers of orange reflect in her vibrant purple eyes. She still cradles her side, but she makes no attempt to rescue Agatha or stop me. My cock softens in response, which I allow, because for the first time, I feel at ease with her being content with me.

The clock ticks as we observe the glory before us.

Minutes turn to an hour.

Agatha's skin bubbles with blisters as we cook

her alive. Her internal organs boil, and in a matter of time they will give out and stop working. The smell of burnt flesh lingers in my nose, and I taste it on my tongue, but I am unbothered.

I step forward and kneel, removing the roaster pan underneath the oven where drippings typically fall, but today it's filled with body juices, burnt strands of hair, and blood. It's hot to the touch, but I am me, and I can do fucking anything. Smiling, I pivot my head to look behind me as an idea comes to me.

And just as I do, Royce breaks the silence we have been submerged in. "How do I know that's true?" she probes. "How do I know you didn't force her to say those things? And how do I know any of this is real?"

Questioning reality, wise sweet girl, but it's far too late for that.

Rising, with the hot pan in hand, I walk over to my naive foster sister and dump the contents of it over her head. Coating her body, the liquid is thick, and once the realization washes over her, a giant scream erupts from her mouth. Her feet move frantically in an effort to escape me, but it's to no avail. Instead they slip on the tile, and her broken body crashes back down to the floor, where she fucking belongs

My head tilts as I take her in. Pathetic. Then it shakes whilst I stand over her blood-soaked body. I drop the pan, and it echoes against the tile whilst I pull the legs of my trousers up. Kneeling, I crouch before her while balancing on the balls of my feet. Harshly, I grip her jaw, spitting out, "Fuck you."

14

ROYCE

My face is buried in the comfort of my pillow while the soft comforter surrounds me, keeping me protected. It took three washes to get the remnants of Agatha off me, but the phantom feeling of her blood coating my body remains. This feeling is tragically familiar; this is how my body aches after *he* uses me. The lingering touches and warm breath across my skin, and the thought sends chills up my spine.

The memory from only hours ago replays in my mind vividly, regardless of whether my eyes are open or closed, and the smell lingers over me. In the moment, as it was occurring, it was as if it were toxic waste, and as he poured it on me, I thought surely I was being burnt alive by a deadly chemical.

Sniffling, my pillowcase soaked in sadness, exhaustion looms as my eyes become heavy, but my mind fights it because it's too dangerous to sleep.

Who am I kidding? It's too fucking dangerous to be awake or even be in this house.

Inhaling deeply through my nose, my mind wanders to impossible possibilities, such as, could I escape? Surely he can't see all or know all.

Already I know I'm dumb for such thoughts, but I continue to humor myself, rationalizing the irrational.

I'm not familiar with his abilities, his powers, and how he is able to grab ahold of me or the others so easily. How he can manipulate our minds to bend to his will. Agatha never allowed us to learn about any magic, just that it exists in our world and that ours was taken from us because we were bad, bad kids unworthy of such gifts.

If only I could find his blind spot.

Frustrated, I think back to our childhood.

The crisp air tickled my skin as I skipped down the cobblestone sidewalks as we explored the town with extreme limitations. Seeing the shops would help expose us to a life our dreams were made of, witches' brew, spell-casting books, and potions. I recall pressing my face against the pane of glass, envying the smiling children with their parents inside. And always thinking, that should have been me with my moms, but as those thoughts occurred, Agatha would pull on the collar of my shirt and remind us we were not the victims because we did this to ourselves. We weren't allowed to argue with her; punishments would be implemented at home if we did. Therefore, I quickly learned to grin and bear it; that was the only technique to keep the peace.

Also, thinking back, Agatha never let me wear my dresses into town. I don't know how I didn't see it then. The manipulation, gaslighting, and suppression had already begun all those years ago, and I was completely fucking blind to it.

I justified it as stern, a strict hand, but it was anything but.

Annoyance festers within me as I shake my head against the pillow, staring at the stark wall.

I've been like this for hours, unmoving. And anytime my eyes attempt to drift closed, all I see is Beckham's dead body in the garden. As the distinct image flashes before me, my body jolts and my eyes shoot open, only to cry some more.

The psychological torture of years past to now, is impacting me to a degree I have never felt before.

Sending my mind and body into autopilot just to survive.

As my brain tingles, exhaustion strikes once more, and I allow it, tired of fighting. I hope it will take me away... far fucking away. Please, make this all end. I'll sit through the memory dump and flooding images of my mate being taken from me if you just allow me to fall into an abyss once done.

Dazed, I continue staring at the bleak wall.

Could this be grief?

I recall being broken when my moms died, but to allow myself time to grieve them properly was never a gift I was given. And now, perhaps, I am grieving all three... or four if we include my childhood, all at once, now.

Then, in a state of unconscious behavior, I feel my heavy, lifeless body roll over. A sharp pain from my ribs begs for me to stop, but I don't, as pain is nothing new to me. Perching myself on the edge of the bed, I take a deep breath in through my nose, waiting for my ribs to calm themselves before glancing over to the wall. And what I focus on is the single most important thing in this room, the fucking window.

It's my only way to salvation.

Pushing myself up, I rise to steady feet, which

heavily move my body across the floor. A sliver of worry attempts to enter me as the loud thuds from the balls of my feet echo, but I push the worry away, deciding if he's going to hear me, he will. There is nothing I can do to stop that now because regardless, I am getting to that window.

My arms wrap around my body as I walk, and I find myself favoring my right side. Feeling around, I try to gauge if my ribs are broken or simply bruised. It's hard to tell, and pushing on them causes me to wince in pain.

The sun still hides behind the dark, swirling clouds. What I would do to just have a taste of sun before it all ended, but I have learned quickly at Agatha Manor that we never get what we want here.

Fingers rise from my torso and grip the wooden windowsill. Sliding it up, I realize it's heavier than I recall, but through the tiniest of cracks, fresh air enters and hope is renewed. I get it up just enough to slide my fingers under to leverage it better. Pushing, the friction of the wood causes it to stick in some spots, making the opening uneven, but it's fucking opening, and that's what matters.

NO!

. . .

PRINCE'S VOICE SURROUNDS ME, and I freeze.

Please don't come. Let me leave, I repeat to myself over and over, pleading for mercy. I am no longer above begging.

He doesn't respond. Silence surrounds me, and I take the chance, continuing my efforts.

But those efforts are short-lived because in one rapid swoop, the window is thrust down swiftly on top of my fingers.

I burst out screaming, followed by a river of tears. The pain is throbbing, and it feels like with each second, they stay trapped. The temperature rises, and they burn red.

Again, my body goes into autopilot and pulls my trapped fingers out from under the thick wood and heavy glass window. The throbbing intensifies, but there is absolutely nothing I can do to alleviate the pain. I release another high-pitched scream; it nearly bursts my own eardrums, leaving them ringing once I am done.

My gaze then wanders to an all-familiar spot, my vanity, and more importantly, the mirror. Moving toward it, I have one goal in mind: it has to work. This is my Hail Mary, my last chance.

I don't bother to make a fist. Instead, I slam my palm against the reflective glass, and a crack fills the room, but nothing breaks. I try again, even harder, and I can feel it breaking under me. On my last thrust, sharp pieces shatter around me to my delight. Reaching for the closest piece, I line it up with a vein that has been taunting me for far too long and go to stab it. But, before I am able to, the glass is quickly whisked out of my grip, and other pieces around me follow.

What? No! Why?

In a matter of seconds, the mirror is as it was, completely whole and unbroken.

"Why?!" I shout, tilting my head to the ceiling and tears flowing once more.

I just want to see my family again.

Instead of responding verbally, the door swings open, catching me off guard. Glancing over, I find the threshold is empty. Unease settles in my bones, and my body tenses.

Hastily, my body is thrown from the safety of my room and down the dimly lit hall. From there, he tosses me down the stairs, ensuring I hit every step forcefully. The edges of the steps jab into my sides and rattle my brain. The pain is immense. Instinct pulls my hands to cover my head, but my hands are fucking useless, aching equally alongside the rest of me.

Reaching the ground on the main floor, my body trembles in shock. I relax into it, and just as I do, he throws me firmly against the front door, where I bounce off it effortlessly, yelping from the impact, before dropping back down to the ground.

Blinking, white spots flash, and stars dance in my vision. My stomach becomes nauseous, and I start vomiting. The human body can only take so much physical abuse and trauma before it revolts, and this is mine screaming for it to end.

The clicking of his dress shoes inch closer and closer. With my vision blurry, I am unable to focus and close my eyes once more. He chuckles. "Your bruises belong to me, as does your body." My body reacts, vomiting more upon his polished shoes.

YOU WILL LIE HERE *and fucking take it.*

I ATTEMPT to move my hands to rise, but the effort is wasted; he's locked me in here. Trapped in a body that won't respond to my brain. His trousers unzip, and dread follows suit. Spitting, I wait for it to land on me, but it doesn't; instead, it's followed by the sound of his cock being worked.

I seek out a distraction, anything, even the large clock ticking, but it's silent.

My mind wanders. How long have I been trapped here?

His voice whispers into my mind, *A while.*

I'm never getting out of here. Forever trapped in a reality that reflects my worst fucking nightmare.

AND ISN'T IT BEAUTIFUL, *my sweet girl?*

TEARS WELL IN MY EYES. *Please just let me die*, I plead shamelessly.

NOW, *where would the fun in that be?*

REALIZATION WASHES OVER ME, and it hits like a ton of bricks. This is all just a game to him, and I am a toy he can do with as he pleases. My resistance toward him no longer matters now that his powers have returned. I am to do what he likes, at his will.

Ear-piercing grunts become louder and louder. His movements are more rapid as his hand

pumps his hard cock.

YOUR NIGHTMARE IS by my design, and your tantalizing screams bring me peace. As I will never let you go.

WITH THE FINAL word penetrating me like a sword to my heart, ropes of his warm cum shoot out of his cock and land directly onto my face. Smiling, he doesn't let up, as if he is decorating me with purpose and precision.

And I have to take it.

Prince's eyes are hooded, and the corner of his mouth twitches in delight as he continues to cover me in his release. Pumping himself faster and harder, he doesn't allow one drop to be wasted or held back. From my face to my hair, his thick cum sticks to me. Then, as it begins to trail off, his last shot lands on my eye, coating my lashes. Stringy, it almost reminds me of a spiderweb.

"Now, get the fuck up; we have a body to bury," Prince barks, standing directly over me, his dick softening and hanging out of his pants. "And don't you fucking dare try cleaning yourself up."

I must not rise quickly enough for Prince because within seconds my body is thrust through the house, to the back door, and then outside, where I land. The fresh air is a welcome guest for my skin and my lungs. The dead grass against my cheek is comforting while the sky still remains dark with circling, looming clouds above.

It doesn't take long for Prince to join me outside. As I hear his footsteps, I look up, and his trousers are done up.

My body is still weak, and on shaking limbs, I slowly rise in absolute agony with my stomach turning.

"You will finish burying her next to your precious vampire..." Looking around, his index finger touches his defined chin. "But wherever could he be?"

A shovel is propelled into my hands, then my shattered fingers are forced around the wooden handle.

Prince shouts one last command before walking away, leaving me with Agatha's blistered body. "Dig!"

Turning my nose up, her body odor is vastly vile. From the melting and burnt skin to blisters and singed hair, I am repulsed as my stomach continues to turn.

HER ROOTS WERE ROMANIAN. It's why her spells weren't familiar to you or me. Your moms loved studying spells and potions from the international witching community, which, ultimately, with your help, killed them.

PRINCE IS SAYING this to hurt me.

But it only motivates me.

I will fucking kill him.

HOURS.

It has been hours now that I have been digging this impossible hole with my broken hands.

And finally, my hands are allowed to release their grip on the wooden handle of my shovel. As it drops to my feet, I am able to hoist myself up from the six-foot hole I stand in.

It takes every ounce of energy and strength to prop myself on the ledge and then bring myself up and over to lie on the yard. My breathing is heavy,

I'm panting, and I wish I could lie here forever with how comfortable I am.

FINISH THE JOB!

AND SUDDENLY I am brought to my feet, standing before Agatha's body.

I use my feet and roll her decaying form, which isn't easy, but I know my fingers won't make it if I use my hands, as they are already fucked up to the point I fear they will never be functional again.

With each kick, she inches closer and closer to the black earth hole. And just as I give her the final nudge needed, Agatha falls to her final resting place.

Sweat mixed with that deranged bastard's cum drips down my face, swiping the back of my hand against my forehead. I steady myself, bracing for yet another punishment for cleaning myself off, but it doesn't come.

Relaxing, I look over Agatha's lifeless body with pride, and I am greeted by a plethora of beautiful gray, black, and white moths fluttering all around me.

Holding my arms out, I let them wrap me in their

embrace. Smiling with joy, this is like nothing I have ever experienced before, and I never want it to end. I yearn for them to perch upon me, to make me their home or friend. To be so comfortable, they put their trust in me.

My toes curl in the earth.

I am happy.

And as quickly as the warmth enters me, my eyes are forced closed once more. And I am welcomed to extreme horror.

Flickers of orange, red, and yellow bounce off my eyelids.

Then, like a movie, the image is blurred, as if it is zoomed in on. I squint, trying to decipher it. It's clearly fire, but I can't tell what's happening. And that's when the movie is zoomed out, and everything comes into clear focus. I gasp. No, please no.

It's Beckham's dead body.

He is tied to a wooden cross, similar to the one that burnt his face, with hot flames dancing around him. And next to Beckham is Prince, who is twisting a sword in his fingers arrogantly. Scanning the area, I know exactly where they are... the front yard.

If only I could get my body to move, I'd get to him, save what's left of my baby, and preserve him forever with me.

My mind races. Why isn't anyone coming to help us? The flames are large, so the smoke surely can be seen from town. *Please, someone help us.*

YOUR PLEAS ARE *of no use here.*

PRINCE THEN DOES THE UNIMAGINABLE. In one fell swoop, his arm rises, and the sharp blade is stabbed into Beckham's neck, and in one clean slice, my vampire's head is removed from his body. My foster brother chuckles, and with my hands still over my gaping mouth, he drops the sword and kneels, gripping Beckham's head by his dark hair, before he rises to his feet proudly once more.

I fall to my knees, trembling in grief.

A STAKE TO THE HEART, *then off with his head.*
   Followed by the burning of the body.
   It's the only way to ensure he stays fucking dead.

THE CRACKLING of the flames against the cross creeps

up Beckham's body, and I slam my fists into the ground.

Screaming "No!" my vision blurs and the painful throb of my headache returns. Everything begins to spin, and nausea returns. My body propels into the black abyss that surrounds me, and internally, I hope this is the end. The thought is ruined when it suddenly stops.

Wide-eyed, I search the area around me, confused, and immediately I know I am back in the safety of my room.

Without hesitation, I lean onto my side and shrink into myself, with my arms wrapping around my bent knees and holding them tightly and painfully into my chest. Silence surrounds me, and I remain here, lying in a state of anxious calm, awaiting the next terrorizing experience to begin.

15

ROYCE

F atigued, my mind finally allowed my body to give in to a deep slumber.

No flashes of haunted memories assault me for once, and instead my eyes were only greeted by darkness, and it welcomed me with open arms. As the darkness fades, light rises, forcing my eyelids to flutter.

Yawning, my arms rise and my legs stretch. My body prepares for the aches and sharp pain to follow, but strangely enough, it does not.

Placing my arms back down next to me, I turn my head in a state of confusion.

"Auk ria, spur notra. Sheeb mortus nor vine. Auk ria, spur notra. Sheeb mortus nor vine." Soft whispers and sharp hisses alert me to the fact I am not alone.

White granulated substances are next to me, and my peripheral vision notices that my hair is now clean, shiny, and fanned out. Flickers of light bounce off the wall, and the warm aroma of candles invades my nose.

Swallowing hard, my breathing becomes heavier as my heart rate speeds. All he would have to do is see my chest rising and falling quicker to know I am awake. But as I wait, no harsh footsteps follow.

My head turns, my neck creaking, and my eyes continue to observe.

"We summon you to protect our own," a strong female voice chants before it all stops. My eyes shift, waiting in this awkward silence, but nobody moves.

Bewildered, my hands attempt to plant themselves firmly on the floor, acting as an anchor so I can rise. But as they are expecting to grip the boards, they fall right past them and are only met with air and space. The fuck?

Panic invades my thoughts, and my legs and feet flail like I am riding an imaginary bike.

I am levitating.

Wide-eyed and shocked, the most polite words that I have ever uttered leave me, "I would like to come down now, please."

Tiny giggles follow before I am left to the silence once more.

With a furrowed brow, my nostrils flare. They changed me; my clothes are different. I am in an ankle-length silk nightdress that is too long for me, delicate gold anklets meet the hem, and my bare feet have toe rings. Moving my gaze up my body, the bruising has vanished, and as I wiggle my fingers, the broken bones are healed.

"And from our dust and ashes to your body and soul, we will survive the night, and their darkness shall never come for us!" Both voices unite and declare in unison, and by the time they reach their last word, my body is safely back onto solid ground.

And with great pride, one of the voices states, "Our baby girl, you are free."

My torso jolts up, my back straight as my breath is swept away from me. Tears are freely flowing. I'm not sure when they started, but I make no effort to control them or stop. Hands tremble, and as I tuck my long, wavy hair behind my ears, my head tilts toward one of the shadowy figures standing behind white candles and the circle of what looks to be salt as she fills in the gap for me.

Making my way up her body, the emotions releasing on the outside are now swelling internally.

White hair and her bright smile greet me.

"Mommy."

She doesn't move, but her face softens. "Yes, baby girl. Mommy is here."

Shaking, the single word trembles out from between my dry lips. "How?"

"The spell's been lifted. The old bitch is dead."

I know that voice.

Nearly giving myself whiplash, my head spins, and before me are a set of bare feet with royal purple toenails that match my eyes. "Mom?" I murmur in disbelief, trying to figure out if this is another game of deception, compliments of my captive. Puzzled, my mind is raddled. Seeing is believing, so I've been told, but these eyes have seen so many lies, it's nearly impossible to differentiate it from truth.

Looking up, her black hair welcomes me home, alongside her mischievous smile.

"She suppressed you, baby girl. Then banished us to a land far away from you. We would try and penetrate through it... and we tried so, so hard."

Mommy's head falls as she comes to stand next to Mom, who comforts her.

Scurrying to my feet, I delicately step over the salt and stand before the two strong women who helped shape me, mold me, and loved me. Another wave of emotion washes over me, and I know I am a blubbering mess, but it doesn't matter. I finally feel whole.

Their faces have the same smile lines and wrinkles, that I proudly gave them. Both sets of eyes bring me comfort and safety, the way they would when I looked for them as a child.

I've missed them so much.

Raising my arms, I go to hug them but stop myself midway as I realize they are here, but they are spirits. Would I just fall through them? I just want my moms. To be overwhelmed by their scents and embrace.

"We can touch you, but you cannot touch us," Mommy tells me as she wraps her hand around my wrist softly before flipping my arm over and calmly asking, without judgment, "Are you okay? What can we do to help?" I don't need to look down to know what she is referencing. My cuts. My scars. Years of unimaginable pain.

Nodding, I respond timidly, "I am now. Don't worry." And it's the truth.

My soulmate is dead. That scar will never heal, but that scar runs deep, invisible, and that is the only one I will pick at daily just to feel him again.

Changing the subject, I say, "What were you

doing to me just now? How am I like this?" I question, confused while trying to take my mind off other things.

"Healing you. He did a number on you, baby girl." Mom pauses, her lips quiver, and her fists ball. "But he will never win."

This is all I have wanted: love, compassion, worry, rules within reason, and respect.

It takes a moment, but Mom's message finally becomes clear. It's ominous and intriguing, and perhaps permission? My brow rises in excitement.

"We also placed a protection spell on you; he nor anyone else can do harm to you anymore. His mind games will no longer work. You hold the power now," Mommy continues where my mom left off. Confused, I don't understand. I hold no power; I have none. It vanished the day they died.

"The curse, the suppression, has been lifted. You are free." Mom reaches forward, her finger glowing white as it pierces through my chest. It's like a ball of energy because I suddenly become hyperaware as her touch warms me. "All you have to do is remember." She says it like it's easy, but it's been well over a decade. "Like guiding lights, you will see. Trees that whimper now dance for thee."

Chuckling, because I must look petrified, "It's

like riding a bike," Mommy jokes, reassuring me as I roll my eyes.

Mom removes her finger from my chest, the glowing ball now missing. Inquisitively I look upon her, but I am only provided with a wink in response.

"This is where we leave you. We promise we will be back. Where you go, we follow. But you must do this part on your own. The reward will be sweeter that way."

I choke up. "But I only just got you back." They can't leave me; I still need them.

Leaning forward, both my moms kiss my forehead and whisper, "I love you," before fading away.

My hands lace through my long locks, growling in frustration. This is so fucking unfair.

"ROYCE!"

My body reacts, freezing in fear.

Prince's voice is like nails on a chalkboard. Rage swells beneath the surface. Closing my eyes, I focus the rage on to remembering, centering the energy to bring me what I need to end this hell I've been living in.

Soft words slither from my lips, words I've not ever spoken before yet feel so familiar as they leave me. "Seeping slowly, bodies tremble. Flickering souls, you are in trouble." Heat radiates from me. I can feel beads of sweat building on my skin. Raising my hands, a purple glow illuminates off my palms, and I'm startled.

"Seeping slowly, bodies tremble. Flickering souls, you are in trouble." I repeat those two sentences, and the flames from the candles extinguish, and the salt, which once surrounded my sleeping body, rises, twisting around me and causing my gown to flutter and my hair to fan out.

Amazed, I don't stop, only building further momentum.

I say it one final time. "Seeping slowly, bodies tremble. Flickering souls, you are in trouble." Flashes of my youth join, moving so rapidly I am barely able to register it all. What I gather is it's moments with my moms, as they would teach me spells and magic. It's my memories flooding back to me. Overwhelmed, I want to scream, but I worry Prince would hear me.

I allow my body to absorb it all. "Please give me strength." I ask shamelessly.

Then, with a final gust, the salt falls, and images fade, but my purple glow remains.

Rushing to my vanity, I bend over and take myself in. "I can't believe it," I whisper to myself. It's like none of this torture ever happened if you were to look at me. My healing process has begun. This is only the beginning, a tiny piece of what it will take, but it helps so fucking much. And then I am caught off guard because of my eyes. Leaning forward, my lashes brush against the reflective glass. My eyes aren't dull anymore; they shine bright with renewed life.

They captivate me.

I am beautiful.

Stepping back, I know I don't have much time, but I take myself in once more in disbelief, then I reassure myself, "It's going to be okay. I'm ready; I can do this."

Feeling confident on my tiptoes, I twirl toward the door and open it without a second thought, because for the first time since my moms died, I finally feel alive.

16

ROYCE

"Scream for your life and tremble for me, as tonight will be your last."

Standing in the darkness of the staircase, I watch Prince. His demeanor is stoic as rhymes flow freely from his poisoned lips. A crystal glass swirls an amber liquid before him, both hands free. His body is slouched, leather shoes resting on the coffee table and crossed at the ankles.

"Say it with me, my sweet sister. Scream for your life..." His voice trails off before coming back with a commanding, "And tremble for me! As tonight..." Leaning forward in the high-back chair, his white eyes meet mine, his tone changes, and each word is said with both purpose and hostility. "...will be your last."

He knows.

He knows, and he isn't going to make this easy.

"Ah, sweet brother, your words are always so comforting," I toy sarcastically while his eyes glare upon me. Steadily, my feet brush each step, calmly, as I make my way to him.

Unamused, Prince returns his focus to his levitating beverage, reaching for it aggressively and taking a swig.

"You appear less damaged than the last time I saw you," Prince states the obvious, baiting me into a battle of words, and I bite, because why not?

"And you look more deranged."

Internally, I am giddy with pride; my confidence has returned, and a renewed sense of hope and purpose flows through my body.

"Yes, killing your boyfriend would do that to a person, don't you think?" His words sting; the pain attempts to overtake me once more, but I resist it because I am not that wounded girl anymore.

Throwing his glass against the dark wallpaper, whatever contents remain splash out as the crystal shatters upon impact.

Being brave, I inch forward onto the shag rug before I'm startled by his sudden movement. His feet hit the ground as his body rises. "I don't need to be a fucking mind reader to know. Your face tells me everything." Prince takes calculated steps forward until his body towers over me, an intimidation tactic I am all too familiar with. "Plus your eyes are fucking glowing." His head tilts, examining me, but I don't cower. "Did your mommies come to save you?"

Ignoring him, my gaze meets his, challenging his dominance. And much to my delight, the corner of his mouth twitches in frustration. *Come on, Prince, give me everything you've got, I am fucking ready.* I challenge him wordlessly while smugly smiling back at him.

Prince tilts his head down, his white hair falling onto his forehead and the tip of his nose brushing against my forehead, while his lips whisper. "Have you ever wanted to get lost in someone so badly you'd kill for it?" His breath reeks of alcohol, and his breathing becomes heavier.

Shaking my head in response, I plainly state, "No." Because it's the truth.

With Beckham, it wasn't about him being my possession or obsession or vice versa. It wasn't about getting lost in him or seeking refuge for a few hours before returning to this hell.

He was my home. I needed him like oxygen. Our

hearts would reconnect the moment our eyes met, and our souls longed for one another when apart.

I would kill for him.

But not because of him.

Prince raises his hand, tucking a piece of my hair behind my ear, and his cock hardens behind his trousers as his body presses against mine. "You were made to hurt, never love."

Seductively, I lick my lips, never breaking eye contact, and whisper back, "And you will always be a fucking child, throwing a tantrum when he doesn't get what he wants."

Through gritted teeth, Prince growls, which only continues to bring me great joy. His cock gets harder against me, and I reach down to cup it, squeezing it tight between my fingers. Hissing, his exposed chest presses against mine. "I love destroying you. Breaking you. Consuming your every thought. Now, why don't you show me your new magic trick?"

My teeth nip his lip, tugging it, piercing through the thin skin until I taste crimson on my tongue. I apply more pressure before releasing him, swiping my exposed teeth with my tongue, taunting him, baiting him.

Squeezing his dick harder, his body jolts in response, and his closed fist slams against the wall behind me. Prince is reaching his limit, the ability to keep himself restrained teetering. He is on the brink. Composure is beginning to break, much to my delight, and my own heart races with excitement. I've never held the power when it comes to him, but now I do, and I am never giving it back.

His Adam's apple bobs, and a piece of me wonders how hard it would be to grasp it and pull it out. How sadistic of me, but I hold no shame; I fucking love it.

"Why aren't you fighting me?"

I laugh devilishly. "Perhaps I already am," I tease cryptically, and Prince doesn't like it. His next statement is meant to provoke, and I love how desperate he is for me to initiate the end, "Your eyes are mine, forever inked into my skin, etched on my bone from now until forever. I own you."

Taking a page out of his book, I muster the courage and spit on his chest. The fist once against the wall is now wrapped tightly around my neck. Squeezing his dick, I remind him who is really in fucking control. Prince's nostrils flare, and my hold over him doesn't make a difference because in one fluid motion, the back of my head bounces off the wall as he pushes me backward.

We have returned to familiar habits.

His free hand cups my pussy through my dress, and my blood boils while my fingertips warm. Glancing down quickly, the purple glow is back, but I remain composed.

"Your eyes always burn so bright for me, baby." If I thought I could, I would launch him through the walls. Only one person can call me baby, and it's not him. But his words, which sting and enrage, don't end, "And I'll slowly skin his mark off your leg, layer by fucking layer, baby."

PENT-UP rage is no longer contained, and I have minimal control and awareness over what comes next. Releasing his cock, both hands rise, while faintly I hear him chuckling as I feel my eyes closing, but this time it's not him forcing it; I am.

"For I am just a vessel which you will never crack. May you live or die with great regret. With turning black clouds and tornado winds, lightning strikes when only one wins. And no one will ever save you." The omen dances off my tongue, and as I spit the word *you*, my eyes flash open.

Prince releases me from his hold, stepping back in amazement with hands raised in surrender, but he's far too late.

My body rises, and my feet hover off the ground.

A crack of lightning sends chills up my spine. It's time.

Looking down at the pathetic sight, a large, bright dome surrounds me, acting like a shield or barrier. Then, everything begins to move in slow motion, and it's captivatingly beautiful.

Still in denial, Prince shouts, "I can never die." His eyes glow wide with hate and anger, not yet accepting defeat.

Shaking arms move before me, and my own scream joins his as a large burst of energy releases from my hands, hitting Prince in the chest. His feet are lifted off the ground, and the force of the impact throws him against the far wall. His body, weak, drops to the ground.

My screaming stops, and the tension increases as his body begins to move. On shaking legs, he rises, using the wall for balance. A black burn mark decorates his exposed chest, and his Adam's apple bobs with each deep swallow.

"Coward," I taunt. My voice has become much deeper than I am used to due to the slow-motion effects. But I don't fight it, allowing whatever has taken over me to be. Prince sees it as an opportunity, making an attempt to catch me off guard and charging at me before springing into the air.

His shoulder braces on one side, ready to spear me. And as he hits my shield, it reacts, and nothing could have predicted its response. My arms, which are still reached out, move to either side of my body, and my chest is pulled forward, rising high as he collides. Bright purple hues illuminate the space as my body trembles. And the house begins to turn to rubble.

The ceiling cracks slowly, and I watch, captivated, before breaking off and plunging to the ground. Dust particles float, and they look like floating stars.

Focusing, I am giving all I have to give. Tears run down my cheeks because I'm scared, and this is overwhelming. The powers which guide me are from my mothers; therefore, I don't fight it. I allow it to keep going until it cannot anymore. But it still scares me, not understanding what I am capable of, but I need to trust they would not lead me astray or give me something I could not handle.

Glancing around once more, looking for *him*, I notice small fires have started. With shaking arms, I feel the energy draining out of me, and time speeds up. My body weakens, but I don't give up. I don't stop until *it's* ready too.

With a final scream, a Hail Mary, and a final burst flows out of me, and a bright white flash is all I see, until tiny flutters surround me.

The magnificent moth has returned. Which means someone is about to die. Perhaps it is me?

The light vanishes, and I tumble to the ground.

Then my vision fades to black.

HEAVY EYES SLOWLY OPEN.

My throat dry, I cough, only to breathe in more smoke and dust. Ears ring as I glance around. My eyes blink slowly while my brain attempts to register what it's seeing. Lying here moments longer, I decide to rise. Rolling from my back to my stomach, I shake my hair, and more dust begins to float around me, causing me to sneeze. Adjusting my body to all fours, I slowly stand still, confused about the current state of where I am... Where am I?

With a furrowed brow, I look down, and my dress is torn and tattered, barely covering the important parts. Walking through the rubble, it's time to explore, my frazzled mind decides. With each step, I keep analyzing the rubble around me. Confused, I am unable to comprehend how I have ended up here. With each step, pieces of debris embed themselves into the pads of my feet. Flashing red and blue lights catch my attention, and I tilt my head, curious, while the ringing in my ears continues.

Looking up, the night sky surrounds us. I allow myself to be captivated by it until I am rudely interrupted.

Startled, voices echo. Looking down, my eyes squint while everything races back, flooding my mind. I let out a deep exhale.

"Ma'am, please come with me," are the first words I hear. A warm blanket follows, being thrown over my shoulders.

"You have been in a horrible accident. You are okay," another voice reassures me. My ankles twist, and I nearly trip while gripping my blanket, and a strong hand grasps my arm to steady me.

Then I stop.

Everyone who is frantic around me watches, not moving. They wait in anticipation, brows raised as my curious mind questions.

"How long has it been?"

A man with a fireman's jacket flutters toward me.

Reading his badge, I note it says *Fire Chief Terry*. "Please, we must get you to the hospital," he insists.

Shaking my head, I decline. "No. Tell me, how long has it been?"

Nobody listens, and bodies resume moving. The man gripping my arm continues to pull me forward even though I resist.

Screaming, as tears flow freely and the adrenaline crash washes over, I say, "Someone answer me!"

Everyone stills, Terry looks petrified, but he responds cautiously. "What do you last remember?"

Squinting, I search my brain for the answer. Beckham coming in me inside the dirty yellow-and-red tent flashes in my head.

"Fright Night."

Terry looks pained.

"Weeks, miss. Weeks."

SOME TIME LATER

His body was never found. It vanished or evaporated; I don't know.

I keep a black candle lit at all times to banish evil and give myself protection.

He will never hurt me again. *He* is fucking gone.

Bronte, my familiar, who is also the cutest tuxedo cat in the world, nudges me, looking for cuddles while I sit in my nook, gazing out at the garden.

After everything, I disappeared. Nurses at the hospital had their backs turned, and I snuck out. As soon as my skin felt the fresh air, I ran and didn't stop running until I reached home.

My childhood home in the woods.

I collapsed. Passing out for hours before waking

again, and when I did, Bronte was by my side, and I knew then that this was right. I would be okay.

With the help of my moms' and magic, we restored the cabin to its original form. Moss covers the roof as vines crawl up the dark wood exterior. Beautiful windows bring the sunshine into my cozy oasis.

Dark wood molding, olive green paint, and built-in shelves and cabinets fill my heart with happiness and childhood memories. A hand-crafted stone fireplace is the highlight of the entire place, and it's where my cauldron hangs. But then there are the shelves upon shelves of leather-bound books with hundreds of years of knowledge within them that I only wish I could consume, and I am trying.

My moms visit often, but they also give me my own space and freedom to grow and learn on my own.

The first time I stepped inside after we put the cabin back together, I raced to the stairs, which led to the lab. They were missing. It's like the stairs were never there to begin with. My moms still protect me even in death, and the feeling of love floods me. Because they didn't want the place where our lives changed to taunt me every day. Removing barriers and giving me an opportunity to find peace—that's unconditional, and it's something I've missed so fucking much.

In the garden, fresh flowers bloom next to my herbs and vegetables. And I make a spot to sit and reflect, to remember my soulmate, Beckham. Vampire lilies mixed in with bluebells and daisies make me smile. He would have loved my eclectic selection in his honor and memory. And at the cabin, my garden flourishes year-round.

Because it's magic.

It's midafternoon, and the fall sun beams through the windows.

It's getting cooler outside, and winter is coming.

With my black cast iron cauldron overtop an open flame, waiting for my herbs to brew, a knock at the door catches me by surprise. Rising from the beanbag chair in my reading nook, where I spend hours upon hours studying all my moms' old books and where I always have my pink candle lit surrounded by citrine crystals, I go to the door and open it. My mind is still reeling from the words I've just read that I didn't even think to check who was knocking.

My eyes widen. Shock trickles through me. The book in my hand drops.

My face goes white, and a loud gasp escapes me.

Some Time Later

Play "Labyrinth" by Taylor Swift

Closing Credits

Lucy.
My Alpha & Beta Team.
The Bat Cave.
Little Bats & Queens.
Tash.
RIP Book Box.
Alina.
Kat.
Harleigh.
Chloe.
Christa.
Rumi.
Daisie.
Nicole.
Chelsea.
Kat.
BrittJoy.
Reggie.
Mariana.
Meme Lord.
Amoy.
Tran.

Maria.

Bianca.

Hope.

Taylor.

Jenny.

Martha.

Kata.

Ria.

Music, My Inspiration.

Stella.

Eggo.

Mr. Kincaid.

Taylor Swift.

Waylon!

Pause song at 1:29

"How?"

Resume song

Pause song at 2:59

"What do you mean? Your house burnt down, and I couldn't find you." His stark white face contorts with confusion and his pearly white canines glisten in the sun, sparkling to match his own skin as I take him in.

My mouth moves, but nothing comes out. Shock is making me speechless.

I force my words out, and at first I stutter. "I... I..." I clear my throat. "I saw it. I watched you die, the forever kind of death." Tears of overwhelming emotion flow. "I was trapped for weeks, hopelessly broken knowing you could never return to me."

"Baby, touch me, feel me. I'm here." He chuckles, confused. "I tried to check on you, but no one was home whenever I would sneak by in the night. I came here often, hopeful, but ended up always disappointed because the cottage remained empty and lifeless until today."

Baffled, I'm finding it difficult to comprehend Beckham's words. Then, it dawns on me.

His mind got into mine, adjusting timelines and my truths. Along with Beckham's, because how could he not see me? I was there the entire time, screaming from the roof as fire danced in the front yard. Dammit!

Perplexed, I decide to stop trying to question it or figure it all out. Because it will take many months to file through it all, piece by piece. To put myself back together.

Wrapping my arms around Beckham's neck, I jump into my vampire boy's arms, my soul no longer fragmented. Temporary pain is lifted. And two beating hearts intertwine.

Resume song

The End.

THANK YOU

A massive thank you to my Alphas and Betas!

Martha 'Amy' Moo Moo

Swizzle

Kata

Tiesha 'T'

Jay 'Boss' Depraved

LUCY! TASH!

And the ENTIRE RIP Family!

Little Bats & Queens!

To the moon and back, I love ya!

xx

Kins

ABOUT THE AUTHOR

Kinsley is a Canadian, Dark Romance Author who dabbles in Taboo, Forbidden, Paranormal and is currently in her Erotic Horror Era. When she isn't plotting her next twisted book or watching true crime docs with her cats, you can find her working for the man. Reading. Or listening to Taylor Swift & Sleep Token.

Make sure you follow Kins on her socials and sign up for her newsletter to see what is coming next!

authorkinsleykincaid.com

Lessons; An Extremely Fucking Taboo Extended Epilogue

Brothers Bond

Fuck Me, Daddy; A Port Canyon Chronicle - Feb 2026

Taboo can be found via the authors' website.

eBooks & Signed Book Shop

Printed in Dunstable, United Kingdom

72494754R00112